The
PLENTIFUL
DARKNESS

⌐ ALSO BY ⌐
HEATHER KASSNER

The Bone Garden
The Forest of Stars

The
PLENTIFUL
DARKNESS

Heather Kassner

HENRY HOLT AND COMPANY

NEW YORK

HENRY HOLT AND COMPANY, *Publishers since 1866*
Henry Holt® is a registered trademark of Macmillan Publishing Group, LLC
120 Broadway, New York, New York 10271 • mackids.com

Library of Congress Control Number: 2020919122

Our books may be purchased in bulk for promotional, educational, or business use.
Please contact your local bookseller or the Macmillan Corporate and Premium
Sales Department at (800) 221-7945 ext. 5442 or by email at
MacmillanSpecialMarkets@macmillan.com.

First edition, 2021 / Designed by Liz Dresner
Printed in the United States of America by LSC Communications,
Harrisonburg, Virginia

ISBN 978-1-25076-400-3
10 9 8 7 6 5 4 3 2 1

For Cameron, who I found when I needed him most

THE MAGICIAN—
QUIETER BY ONE

Gloom cluttered the whole of the tower, and within its dark folds stood a magician. She wore a grim smile and an ink-black suit. Both cut severe lines, softened only by the tendril of fog that plumed from her mouth.

The magician swirled her hand through the air. The fog tightened and heavied, it twisted and reshaped, and at last, it settled around her shoulders, the smokiest of magical cloaks. One that held close *the quiet*.

But it was not enough.

Beyond the tower, the village of Warybone and all the people within it breathed. In and in, and out. So loudly.

How dare they, she thought.

Her pulse thundered against the black ribbon she wore cinched at her throat. She stalked to the window and threw back the shutters. Glaring out at the town and the black sea beyond it, she cursed each chimney spiraling smoke, each moonlit lamp shining in a cottage window, each couple strolling down the lane.

"Hush," she hissed to the night, wishing to smother it in a cloud of silence, to dim the candle glow until everything below the tower glimmered black.

With a whoosh of her cape, she turned from the window. Moonlight flooded the circular room, betraying every quiet space and exposing the beamed walls, which rose like a rib cage of brittle bones.

Across from her, a stairway descended into the belly of the tower. She alighted down the twisted steps. Around and around, lower and lower, she went, skipping fastest past the locked door on the third story. Cobwebs clung to the corners of the frame, evidence of how long she'd left it closed.

As she stepped into the street, the magician pulled up her hood, concealing her raven-wing hair and her narrow face, which was best kept out of sight so as not to scare the children. It wouldn't do much good if they ran from her before she could catch them.

A chill filled the magician's bones. It felt like winter instead of autumn, though all the pumpkins displayed on the porches and stoops told her otherwise. Lights flickering, their jack-o'-lantern faces leered at the magician, but at least they were silent.

Striding by, she murmured under her breath, and the pale moon-blue flames winked out one by one. The townsfolk would think it was the wind and nothing more.

Or the rain.

The tiniest drops had begun to fall. They struck the street, the rooftops, the bramble. But they did not touch the magician, not even when the rain poured heavier from the sky. She commanded it away from her the way she might sweep back a curtain.

As she glided farther down the hill, she touched the silken scarf in the pocket of her suit coat, rubbing her thumb over its seamless fabric. The scarf was darker than night, softer than air. It brought her equal amounts of comfort and pain.

Gently, she pushed it deeper into her pocket.

At the same moment, a shrill, grating noise ripped through the night. The magician stumbled, pressing her hands to the sides of her head. She cowered in her cloak of quiet, but it could not ward off this awful sound.

With widened gray eyes, she looked all around, seeking its source.

She had to silence it.

Ahead of her, on a rather flat stretch of the hill, a row of quaint houses sat beneath the clouds and rain. They looked much too tidy to hold such a sound, but there was no question it originated here.

And here it would end.

A flicker of movement caught the magician's eye. She slowed.

Someone stood there in the rain, tight to the little white

cottage at the very end of the row. The figure dared to breathe. Of course it breathed. In and in, and out.

But it was not the source of that wretched commotion.

One thing at a time, she thought. Her focus turned from the small snooping body beneath the window to the shrieking disharmony churning from within the walls of the cottage. Whoever conjured the noise, that's the one she wanted firstly.

The magician waited, dry beneath the stormy sky. At last, the sound cut off. At last, the rain stopped. At last, the snooping figure peeled away from the house, running, running right past where the magician stood. She could have reached out one white hand and snatched the child's skinny wrist.

But not now. Not yet.

"You'll have your turn." The cloak of fog masked her words as the dark-haired child fled, unaware of how close it had come to the magician—and the ever-dark night that awaited anyone she touched.

The magician took a step toward the house, bracing herself should the pitiful sound crash down again. An ache beat at her temple. She'd spent too long in the streets of Warybone. Too long away from the tower. It hurt, it hurt *awfully*, these sounds pounding in her head. (And in her heart.)

But the streets would soon be quieter by one.

1

THE LUNAR MIRROR

A Few Hours Earlier

Stardust was trickier to catch than moonlight. In fact, Rooney de Barra had never caught a speck of it. It danced far out of reach, little gems in the evening sky that taunted her with their bright sparkling.

Even on overcast nights like this one, they glittered through the gray.

Standing in the darkened alleyway, Rooney ran a thumb over the round metal case in her hand—the exact size of her small palm. A thorny stem was etched on the lid, and she cracked it open. It might have looked like a chainless pocket watch, but nestled within lay a very special mirror.

A lunar mirror.

Some said these rare mirrors were made from the moon itself, tiny slivers of the dead rock fallen to Earth. Rooney thought that notion silly, because she knew the truth.

Magic touched the glass.

Oh, it was a most extraordinary mirror. The silvery surface rippled like the sea, then settled smooth and shiny once again. She tucked her dark hair behind her ears and tipped her face over the glass. Her freckled white cheeks, her arrowed eyebrows, and her bark-brown eyes left no reflection.

The only face the mirror would reveal was that of the moon.

Rooney polished the glass with the frayed sleeve of her coat, checking for nicks or scratches, removing fingerprints and thumb smudges. When she was through, the mirror shone.

Its reflected light exposed the blackened bricks of the buildings to each side of her, the grime-coated windows, and the mold stuck in the cracks. Rooney wrinkled her nose and inched away from the walls so she stood in the very center of the alleyway.

A thread of silver fell between the old buildings and glanced upon her cheek. She took one step back, and another half step, lifting her right arm and holding it steady with the left. Quite precisely, she angled the mirror toward the sky. It reflected the dark clouds above and sieved a smidgen of moonlight, which spiraled down through the air, wispy and blue.

Rooney held very still so the mirror would not tilt. One little twitch might spill the light instead of capture it, and she needed every last drop.

A breeze swept by, scampering through the alley and swooping up, up, up into the sky. Rooney kept her feet firmly planted. Her raised arm never wavered. But the clouds shifted when pushed, and the moon disappeared behind them.

She frowned, turning the mirror this way and that, but it did no good. The moonbeams could no longer reach her.

And of course, the stardust only teased her, a glimmer beyond the fog.

Rooney closed the mirror and tucked it into the pocket of her long coat. With a huff, she stalked down the alleyway. It was undoubtedly the worst place to catch moonlight, but it was the one place in Warybone she felt safest.

Yes, it was dark. (Very.) Yes, it was crooked and foul and dank. (Very, very, very.) But it was quiet too. A hushed space that Rooney had all to herself.

Or mostly.

The rats gathered here too. Thick furred and long tailed, they skittered through the shadows, unbothered and right at home. No one troubled them in the alley. No one shrieked or kicked them out of the way like the gents and ladies and roughhouse boys did in the cobbled streets. All those hard-knuckled boys scared of getting bitten, while Rooney slept beside the little beasts without suffering a single scratch or nibble.

In unspoken agreement, the Montys—which was what she called the rats, a collective name for all of them, as she could hardly tell one hairy creature from another—behaved quite politely, and she offered them the same courtesy.

She could not say the same for the roughhouse boys. She'd rumbled with them a time or two. They were all bruises and teeth.

Rooney watched for them now (the boys, not the rats) as she emerged from the alleyway and hesitated on the darkened street. At each corner, lamps glowed blue in the misty air, moonlit sparks wavering behind the glass, and within each house, moonlit flames leaped in the hearths, for when moonlight touched wood or wick, it warmed, and when it touched metal or glass, it cooled.

It was much safer than the outdated use of fire or gas, which could as easily warm a house as burn it to the ground. Spilled moonlight would only glimmer harmlessly before it eventually faded away.

She cast a look over her shoulder. Usually the boys made enough noise in their coming that she heard them before she saw them, but it was still wise to be cautious.

Her boots fell softly on the street as she crept forward. One of the Montys followed her the length of a block and then another, keeping close to her ankles. It was a skinny thing (like Rooney herself) with a scruffy black coat and a splotch of white on its nose.

Rooney glanced up at the sky. She licked her finger and held it out in front of her, trying to gauge which way the wind would carry the clouds. That-a-way (she did not know north from south), she guessed, and turned left down Cider Street.

Best to stay on the busier avenues as long as she could, where the laughter and music from the taverns spilled out into the night. (At this hour, there were still more smiles than fists.)

The Monty continued to follow her. It must have felt safe in her shadow, hoping she'd spare a crumb. One it wouldn't have to fight over with its sharp-toothed brothers and sisters.

"I've got nothing for you, I'm afraid." Her stomach grumbled. "And nothing for me, unless I gather a mirror-full of moonlight to trade for my supper."

It was probably only a shadow falling across its snout, but the rat seemed to frown.

"As though you could do any better in weather like this," she scoffed, then sighed. "If only I could figure out how to capture stardust, I'd never go hungry again."

If moonlight gleamed like glass, starlight would glitter like diamonds.

And like diamonds, it would be worth so much more.

Both forms of light could be cut and shaped into sparkling necklaces and delicate rings; into golden or silver-blue thread, ribbon, and rope; into glinting ever-lit chandeliers. But whereas moonlight was fleeting, starlight was forever.

At least, that's what all the stories whispered in the streets of Warybone told.

Rooney wasn't sure about all that, but gathering a twinkling from the stars above would prove a thing or two to those roughhouse boys. That she was as good as them.

That she was *better* than them. For they'd never caught a bit of starlight either. They would beg her to show them how she'd done it.

"One day," she muttered.

Rooney kicked a stone in her path and stuffed her hands into her pockets. Thistle Hill stood in the distance. The highest point in all of Warybone, it was the perfect place for catching moonlight, but it was also the spot the roughhouse boys had claimed as their own.

She would just have to avoid them as best she could.

The Monty followed her up the narrowed street, its little claws scratching over the stones. Rooney's eyes flicked to the Tower of Thistle, rising dark and straight into the night. The roof shimmered.

"Do you think the stories are true? That starlight sturdies the tower?" The rat made no reply and only slipped closer to her heels. "Well, *I* think it's true. Come on."

The hill inclined slowly, with cottages sitting crooked on its slope. Where the land was too rocky or the hill too steep, blackberry bushes grew untamed, and in these open spaces Rooney felt most wary.

Maybe the Monty did too. It skittered away, as if something had scared it off. Rooney froze. A tap-tap-tapping pelted the cobblestones. She looked all around, ready to dart off after the rat.

Then a scraping sound split the night. Rooney trembled.

After all, these days there were even worse things on the streets than the roughhouse boys.

2

KINDLING

Worse things.

Rooney did not want to think about that now. It was only a story anyway—the thing that was disappearing children from the streets of Warybone come dark fall.

A breeze struck her all at once. Cold, wet pinpricks speckled her cheeks.

With a startled gasp, she fled. Just ahead sat a row of cottages. She darted toward the nearest one, crowding close to its wall, but she had not been as fast as the whip-tailed rat in her escape.

The sky grumped gray, dumping rain. Rooney was already soaked through and through. She swiped a hand across her face, pushing back wet strands of hair.

Slouched under the dripping eaves, Rooney glared into the ever-darkening night.

She pressed herself more firmly against the rough wall of the house, folded her arms across her chest, and waited impatiently for the rain to stop. But it continued to fall.

Rooney sidled closer to the front window. Her tall boots squelched in the mud as she rose to her tiptoes and leaned forward. Through a crack in the shutter, Rooney peered into a formal sitting room.

Against the far wall, a moonlit fire blazed blue in the hearth, two straight-back chairs flanking it. A trim, broad-shouldered woman with dark brown skin perched on one. Her foot tapped the floorboards. A bearded, bespectacled man sat cross-legged in the other. His tapered brown finger drummed the brim of his pipe. Grinning, they looked, not at each other, but toward the corner of the room.

Rooney smooshed her face against the shutter. Even so, she could not see what they gazed at so fondly, and she could not understand what made them smile in such a manner.

Not with that horrible whining sound piercing the night.

It came from this room. It cut right through the rain. All the town must have heard the shrill, scraping sound, worse than graveyard cats yowling and hissing and spitting.

Rooney frowned. She covered her ears. But she kept stubbornly in place, not wanting to get any wetter than she already was.

With one final shriek, the sound quieted. The man and the woman clapped their hands softly. From the corner of the room came the shuffle of footsteps, and then a girl, who couldn't have been any older than Rooney's twelve years, strode forward.

She held a violin and bow.

Rooney blinked. Never had she known an instrument could make such a dreadful sound. The girl hadn't been playing the violin, she'd been *torturing* it.

The girl bowed at the waist, first to her mother and then to her father. The tail of her black braid swung over her shoulder, and her brown cheeks rounded in a smile when their clapping continued.

Rooney would have clapped along with them (not in appreciation, only thankful for the quiet), but of course, she did not want to give herself away—a girl clinging to the wall of a house the way a river leech suctioned itself to skin.

So she turned back around and resumed glaring into the night. Her boots sank deeper into the mud, as heavy as her mood.

She was not thinking about how she missed having a mother and father of her own (though she did miss them very much). She was not thinking about how wonderful it might be to play an instrument (horribly or otherwise). All she was thinking about was how toasty this family must have been before the hearth, while she stood shivering in the rain. If she'd been bolder, she would have snatched the violin from the girl's unskilled hands, as she could have put it to better use than the girl had.

It would have made excellent kindling for a fire.

But though the disused heat source might warm her, it would not fill her stomach, and she'd yet to catch enough moonlight for supper. She pulled her mirror from the pocket of her coat, eyeing the clouds and wishing them away.

Around her, the rain fell softly, and then softer still. Before she could break away from the house and be on her way, the shutters beside her flew open. She ducked, but too late. The shutter on the right smacked against the house, and the one on the left knocked against her head. She yelped, rubbing the tender spot on her temple (but she supposed she deserved it for poking her nose where it didn't belong).

The woman she'd spied through the window turned wide eyes on Rooney. Her hands flew to her face, covering cheeks, nose, and mouth. She screamed, stumbling away from the window and into her husband's arms.

"Someone's outside!"

Small as she was, Rooney must have looked a fright. Dirt-spattered clothes, hair wet and flattened on her scalp, a grimace twisting her lips. She edged away from the house, tramping mud as she went. Rooney didn't want to be scolded for snooping, or worse, handed over to Warybone's warden.

"Who's there?" the man called. He came no closer to the shutters, kept in place by his wife's clawed grip.

The girl, however, hurried forward. No longer carrying

the violin, her fingers curled around the frame. She squinted into the dark-pinched night, but Rooney had reached the edge of the yard and stood beyond the blue light glowing from the window, holding her mirror tight.

"Come away from there, Devin."

"In a minute," the girl said.

Her eyes crawled across the night and settled on the spot right where Rooney stood. Rooney would have darted away, but any sudden movement might have drawn the girl's attention. Instead, she hunched her shoulders, tucking her hands to her chest. Without meaning to, she squeezed, thumb pressing down. The mirror's case clicked open.

At the same time, the thinnest crack parted the clouds. Moonbeams fell gently. A frail spark of light glanced off the mirror's surface like a startled moth. Scowling, Rooney snapped the case closed, and the pale shimmering winked out. She held very still, hoping the girl's eyes would travel past her.

The girl leaned farther out the window, as if she might swing her legs over the frame and climb through it. Her lips parted.

Rooney squirmed. She held her breath.

"No one's there, Mother," the girl shouted back, although she must have spotted Rooney. A fat drop of rain plunked down from the eaves onto her head, and she ducked back inside, passing a hand over her hair.

Rooney's legs wobbled in relief.

Only for a moment, though.

The girl no longer watched her from the window, but the shiver tunneling down Rooney's spine told her that *someone* still did.

3

THE ROUGHHOUSE BOYS

ooney spun around. A splotch of darkness, deeper than the rest of the night, shadowed the air beside her. It drifted closer. A strange presence hidden in a cloak of fog. She flinched away from the unseen eyes that most surely watched her. A cold prickle touched her skin, and she ran, as if something chased her.

Up the hill she dashed, then Rooney skidded to a stop on the rain-slicked cobblestones. She'd reached the spot she'd meant to find, a small slope high above Warybone, so thick with thorns and greenery, and so near the tower, she'd thought it too creepy for the roughhouse boys to gather.

But there they were, the four of them clogging the hillside.

She sucked in a breath. The air was thinner here, the lights from the houses down below faded in the fog. Not a single candle shone from the tower's shuttered windows, not even from the one flung open, staring down at Rooney like a dark, unblinking eye.

Three of the boys stood up to their waists in a patch of long grass and overgrown blackberry bushes. They looked at the sky and the clouds drifting past, elbowing one another out of the spot where they thought the moonlight would tumble.

But one boy stood apart from the rest, balanced up in the branches of an oak, where he was closer to the sky. Even with so many hours left in the night, he'd probably already collected all the moonlight he needed, his mirror full to the brim.

This thought, more than the hard look on his white, dirt-streaked face, bristled against Rooney the most.

Trick Aidan was always besting her.

He scrambled to the ground, quick as a squirrel, then cocked his head to the side, staring straight at Rooney. A smug smile turned up the corner of his mouth, as if he knew just what she was thinking. She glared at him—at his black hair brushing his chin (all messy and wet), at his eyes (as dark and sour as blackberries), at his sharp-knuckled fists already raised. He might have been as wiry as Rooney herself, but the very bones inside him formed harder lines.

Rooney pushed back her shoulders and pressed her lips together. Dripping wet, she couldn't have been any more intimidating than the smallest of the Montys, but it was the toughest face she had and she wore it like stone—unflinching and cold.

Trick sliced his way through the brambles and stepped into the street, blocking Rooney from racing up the hill. She was quick. She might have outrun him, but the winding road led only to the stardusted tower.

A dead end.

Trick rolled his shoulders, shaking water from the worn collar of his coat. "What are *you* doing here?"

"What do you think?" Rooney flashed the mirror in her hand. No sense in hiding what was so obvious.

"Here?" he said snidely, a reminder that she trespassed.

Her heel lifted. His clipped voice almost drove her back, but it would have been far worse to retreat, so she stepped forward instead. "Yes, here, if I want to."

His eyes narrowed. As if he might push her down the hill himself, he too took one step closer.

And so did the rest of the roughhouse boys. Their heads swung all at once, long necks stretching to see her better. The bushes rustled and twigs broke as they crushed through them. Grim smiles stretched across their faces, for Rooney knew the only thing they might have liked better than catching moonlight was keeping her from taking it.

As for Rooney, no one was there to sneak out of the shadows and stand shoulder to shoulder beside her. She had no friends (rotten or otherwise).

"Who's that sogging all over our streets?" The question

came from the smallest, and the toughest, of the rain-soaked pack.

Bridget Mullen.

The girl was a roughhouse boy through and through. Mean and brave and quick wristed with her mirror when catching moonlight. She had a slash of dark hair snipped straight across her eyebrows and her collarbone, and skin so pale she must have avoided spending any time in the sun. Across the corner of her mouth, a thin scar puckered like a too-small fish that had been caught on a line and thrown back into the river.

"Looks like she's half-drowned," the girl said.

"Am not," Rooney grumbled under her breath. Oh, how she hated the way they made her squirm.

Bridget shoved one of the boys out of her way and stalked to Trick's side. Half a foot shorter than him, she stood almost exactly eye to eye with Rooney. But Rooney felt so much smaller, just one girl alone.

"Ah, Bridge," a blond-haired, pale-skinned boy called Sim said with a snicker. "It's Ratty de Barra."

Rooney stole a quick look at the ground, fearing the smudge-nosed rat had returned and wound around her ankles. (It hadn't; it wasn't.) *"Rooney,"* she said, though of course they already knew and didn't care.

Bridget let out a low-pitched laugh, and the rest of them joined in.

A boy named Colin came even with Bridget. He had a

boyish face with wide eyes and soft brown cheeks, but that didn't fool Rooney. She knew he was as terrible as the rest of them, even if he had a quieter way about him. "We don't like your sneaking."

"Don't care." Besides, Rooney was hardly *sneaking*. She'd walked straight up the old road.

"We don't like your face," Sim said.

"Don't. Care." Rooney hadn't seen her face in a good while since the only mirror she owned wouldn't reflect it. She had no doubt it was as long and thin as the rest of theirs and wasn't so pretty to look at with all the grime, so it was hardly an insult.

"We don't like *you*," Bridget snapped.

This wouldn't have wounded Rooney (after all, she didn't much like them either), but Trick looked away then, his face upturned to the sky, as if he couldn't be bothered with needling and torturing her. As if she were such a small thing, pesky as a rat, and *beneath* needling and torturing.

Rooney huffed. She glared. Her mouth opened, but she had no comeback.

Bridget's green eyes flashed, and *she* had no problem finding the words she wanted. "Payment is due." Her hand shot out.

Rooney thought Bridget meant to smack her and took a step back before she could stop herself. As soon as she did, she knew it was a mistake.

"These are our streets. This is our moonlight." Bridget's

little scar stretched as she smiled—her kill look. "Give it." Her open palm waited.

She could only mean one thing: what Rooney held most dear. What she'd *never* give anyone. The only thing that brought her any joy.

Her mirror.

"You're making her cry, Bridge," Trick said.

Only Trick would sink so low. "The *rain* is in my eyes," Rooney sputtered.

Unmoved, Bridget wiggled her fingers. "I said, *give it!*"

"No."

Bridget smiled wider, a signal that this small defiant response pleased her. "Then we'll just have to *take* it. Get it, boys."

1

THE ALLEY OF RATS

Rooney fled down the hill toward Warybone.

Behind her, the roughhouse boys' boots smacked on stone. They didn't holler or shout or call after her, and it seemed less a game, then, without their jeering voices echoing in the night. They chased her with eagle-eyed focus.

In her rib cage, Rooney's heart knocked all around. She couldn't let them catch her. She couldn't let them take her mirror.

Hair streaking behind her, she charged down Cider Street. She slipped her way through the crowd stumbling in and out of the tavern, hoping the boys would lose sight of her or be collared and scolded for running the streets too boldly.

At the corner, she chanced a backward glance and caught sight of Colin, Sim, and Bridget. She looked all around for the fourth roughhouse boy, but Trick, who she'd thought would be at the front of the pack, most eager to catch her, was nowhere to be seen. Rooney grinned.

One down.

A glimmer of hope flickered inside her, as if a blue moonlit flame burned in her chest. She cut left, then left again and again and again, making a full turn around the block because they wouldn't expect her to take such a simple route rounding back on itself. She whipped her head to the side, grinning wider when she saw that Trick was well and truly gone, and Sim too. Only Colin and Bridget remained.

Two down.

Rooney ran faster, winding deeper through the city until her lungs ached and her feet too, loose pebbles pressing into the worn soles of her boots. Eventually, she began to slow, to tire, but not to give in. Just before rounding the next corner, she took a quick look back, and what she saw—Colin stopped and panting in the middle of the street far, far behind—sent a burst of energy through her limbs. She pumped her legs harder.

Three down.

Only Bridget remained, and Rooney had a plan.

She swung that-a-way back toward her alley, racing there directly instead of trying to lose Bridget with twisty turns. Laughter rumbled in Rooney's throat as she returned to the place she knew best.

"Hello, Monty," she gasped, greeting the wet, beady-eyed

rat that sat at the mouth of the alley. It swiped tiny paws over its whiskers, and another rat came to join it, this one even larger and more snaggletoothed.

All the better, Rooney thought, for everyone feared something, and what Bridget Mullen feared was *rats*. Bridget's too-big mouth had once let out this secret. Rooney would never be so careless with her own.

Rooney darted into the darkness, then watched the entrance to the alley, tensed in case Bridget charged through it after her. The slap of footsteps came closer and closer. The shadowed outline of a figure blocked the way out.

A shriek rang loud in Rooney's ears.

The rats must have greeted Bridget too.

Bridget Mullen had lost a finger to one—or so she said—and oh, how she'd moaned over its loss. All for something so insignificant. Only the very tip of Bridget's pinkie went missing, after all. A layer or two of pink skin scraped off somehow (chomped off, according to Bridget).

True or not, Rooney had never been more thankful for the rats.

"Come out of there!" Bridget shouted into the dim, but she did not cross from the street into the alleyway. Her silhouette slipped back and forth as she paced.

"I won't," Rooney called back. "And *you'd* better get out of here, unless you want to lose another finger!"

The rats squeaked and skittered about, disrupted by the loud voices. Bridget kicked at their sleek bodies, hopping from foot to foot to get out of their path. She slunk away from the opening, breathing hard, hands balled into tight fists.

Her voice lowered. "That mirror is ours now. We'll have it, this day or another."

Rooney clutched the silver case. "It isn't; you won't. *Neither* this day nor another."

She waited and listened, braced and ready to pounce should Bridget brave the alley of rats. Bridget said not another word. She only stood there glaring, until at last, with a great huff, she stormed away.

Rooney let out a sigh of her own. Her muscles, all bunched up in her neck and legs, relaxed, and she thought she might collapse.

Leaning against the old brick wall, Rooney looked down at the mirror still in her hand. It was right where it belonged and right where she'd first found it. One lonesome night she'd fallen asleep and in the morning, there it was, the mirror lying in her palm. Something so rare and beautiful and promising when everything around her had gone wrong and rotten.

That's how she knew the mirror was magic. Like an impossible wish made upon a star, it had come out of nowhere when she needed it most.

Tonight, she might have been without supper, but she would not be without her mirror. It was the only thing that mattered.

Something shuffled at the end of the alley.

"Settle down, Montys. That awful girl is gone."

The rustling came again. Whispered steps edged forward. *Foot*steps, not the pitter-patter of little rat paws.

And then a figure was atop her. A quick hand lashed out and snitched the mirror from her fingertips.

"My mirror!" Rooney cried.

The figure danced away from her. Moonlight slivered between the clouds, catching on a pale face.

Trick Aidan.

Burrs clung to the hem of his long black coat. Scratches scuffed his boots. But the most tattered thing about him was the expression he wore, a ragged grin. "What took you so long?"

Rooney thought she'd lost him in the chase, but she should have known better. He'd guessed where she would come. All he had to do was head here directly and wait for her arrival.

Catching her off guard when she thought she was finally alone.

She took a swipe at him. "Give it back!" Rooney's voice rose in panic. She snatched at his arms with fists and nails. She wanted to tear right through him and take back her mirror. "It's mine!"

Trick dodged her blows, shielding the mirror in his hands. "You know where to find it," he said, and bolted.

On legs wobbling from running, Rooney stumbled after

him. She reached for his coattails, but before she could grab them, she tripped—on a meddlesome rat, no doubt—falling to the ground.

In defeat, she lifted her head, only to see Trick streaking into the night, too fast, too far ahead for her to catch him.

5

THE WORST OF
THE WORST

When morning dawned, Rooney wanted to pull the
night sky back over her head as she would a blanket. For all she'd wished, wished, wished upon the
evening stars, her lunar mirror had not miraculously returned
to her.

It stabbed at her heart. That she'd lost—*that she could not
protect*—her lunar mirror. It was irreplaceable. No shop in
town sold its likeness, and no ordinary mirror held its magic.
Trick Aidan had bested her again.

Although this theft did not hurt as much as it had when
she'd lost—*when she could not protect*—her parents, it brought
their absence more sharply to her mind. Trick had swept into
the alleyway, quick and merciless, snatching away her mirror,
just as the feather flu had flown into Warybone last year,
taken root in those townsfolk with vulnerable lungs, and
stolen her parents' final breaths.

Like she had that first night without her mother and father, Rooney felt empty inside.

She curled her fingers into fists and kicked her wooden crate where she slept, knocking a slat loose. And then she turned down the alley and walked out into the dawn-blushed street.

Sunlight rippled in the puddles, all golden and lovely. Rooney stomped through them, eyes focused straight ahead. That smudgy Monty followed, clicking along beside her. She eyed it suspiciously. "Haven't you got anything better to do?"

But it mustn't have; it didn't.

At the edge of Warybone, right before the wilder lands took over, ran a little stream bordered with thorny blackberry bushes. Rooney ate fistfuls of the overripe fruitlets, drank her fill of the cool water, and scrubbed some (but not nearly enough) of the grime from her skin and her clothes.

And all the while, she plotted her revenge on Trick Aidan. The Monty, its pointy teeth nibbling on a blackberry, was surprisingly good at listening.

"I'll take back my mirror, and I'll take his too. It would serve him right, wouldn't it?" Rooney plucked a long piece of dried grass from the earth and wove the wheat-white blade through one of the many holes in her stockings. "Oh, he's the worst of the worst!"

The Monty chittered, a scratchy sound that would have sent Bridget Mullen running.

"Good point. Bridget shouldn't go unpunished. But first

things first. My mirror above all else." Rooney cinched the blade of grass, shrinking the hole in her tights, and knotted the sharp ends.

The Monty blinked in what must have been agreement, and Rooney stood, testing out her make-the-most-of-it stitching. "Now, where might they be?" She regarded the Monty. "Can you sniff them out for me?"

The Monty's tail whipped to the side. Rooney turned, gazing ahead, as if the rat had pointed purposefully. "Come on, then." She clomped forward, her nose following the scent of sausages and coffee and fresh-baked bread.

All the roughhouse boys would be slopping up breakfast, most likely, especially if they had a little extra moonlight to sell and moonstones to spend now that they had Rooney's mirror too.

But they won't have it for long, she promised herself.

In the streets beneath Thistle Hill, the townsfolk bustled about. "Keep close," she warned the Monty, eyes scanning the shopfronts and alleys for any sign of the boys.

Usually she did all she could to avoid them. It was a strange thing, to be searching them out instead.

Halfway down the next block, she froze all at once. A low-pitched laugh that could only belong to Bridget Mullen carried on the air.

Rooney ducked to the side, pressing close to the cold bricks of the hat shop's wall. She looked down the street, and there at the corner stood Bridget, Trick, Sim, and Colin.

They each held a small loaf of soda bread. It *steamed*, still warm from the oven. A growl rolled through Rooney's stomach, never mind that it was full of blackberries.

In the shadow of the awning, she inched closer. Oh, she wanted to march right up to them, but she had to be sneakier about it than that. She was outnumbered, outfisted . . . but she would not be outsmarted.

She stared at the boys and the roundness of their cheeks as they chewed the bread, wishing it was just as easy to see the lump of her mirror in one of their pockets. Trick might still have it, or he might have handed it off to Bridget.

All day she followed them, and though weary of spying, Rooney allowed herself to creep closer still. The Monty hurried to catch up and slipped too near the heel of her boot. Rooney stumbled, her feet smacking loudly against the cobblestones. The Monty squealed and dashed off.

Ahead, Trick went still. Then, whip-fast, he turned toward Rooney.

She leaped into the nearest doorway and huddled in the narrow entry. Surely he couldn't see her here.

But his eyes probed the shadows. They latched onto Rooney.

He came no closer, only slipped his hand into his pocket and pulled out *two* mirrors. One after the other, he tossed them into the air. Rooney felt sick at the thought of him dropping her mirror, of the glass shattering. Nothing would be worse. He juggled sloppily, trying to tempt her from her hiding spot, before tucking them back into the folds of his coat once again.

Rooney's fingers dug into the door frame. She glared daggers at Trick.

Bridget tugged Trick's sleeve, and when he turned back to his friends, they continued down the street, laughing beneath the rising moon.

Rooney stepped out of the doorway. A cool breeze wailed past, fluttering a single sheet of paper stuck up on the storefront window.

Her eyes caught on the weatherworn page. She leaned closer, flattening it against the glass so she could see the whole of it.

A familiar face stared back, sketched in charcoal with a careful hand. Soft eyes, round cheeks, one long dark braid. The girl from the cottage window. The girl with the violin.

Beneath the portrait, written with a shaky hand, was a plea for the return of *the very dear, the deeply loved, Devin Hayes*.

For a moment, Rooney forgot about her mirror. This poor girl, who she'd seen only one evening past, had gone missing, snatched away by the thing in the streets even worse than the roughhouse boys.

A chill swept through Rooney. Not as sharp and cold as the one she'd felt outside the girl's house, but one that tickled her bones all the same.

Rooney glanced away from the paper, turning back in

the direction the roughhouse boys had gone. Already, they'd slipped out of sight. She took a step forward, toward Thistle Hill.

But she hesitated. The lampposts flickered with moonlight, and darkness settled more heavily as evening fell.

She did not like the idea of being alone in the streets at night (without even the Monty beside her for company), for if she too was taken, no one would tack up a poster begging for her return—no one at all would know she was gone.

6

BLACKTHORN

Later that night, steeling herself against her worries, Rooney hid in the bushes at the base of Thistle Hill. Now was not the time to feel sorry for herself. She refused to let the darkness (and whatever existed *within* the darkness) scare her, and so she waited for the roughhouse boys.

On a clear night like this one, moonlight would practically fall into the lunar mirrors. She didn't know what was taking the roughhouse boys so long. She'd have finished already, she was sure of it, and despite her otherwise grim mood, she warmed with pride at her moonlight-catching abilities.

Those boys didn't know what they were missing when they'd turned her away from joining them.

"I didn't want to be one of them anyway," Rooney whispered to the Monty, who had curled up beside her among the roots and mulch.

The rat twitched its nose. It mustn't have believed her.

"I didn't; I don't." Rooney stretched out her legs and poked at one of the unpatched holes in her stockings. "Have you already forgotten how horrible they are?"

The Monty climbed to its feet and scampered across her knees. It peered out at the winding road ahead.

Rooney quieted.

She listened.

Oh yes, she usually heard them before she saw them, and right then, the roughhouse boys were fast approaching, as if the soles of their boots were made of bricks instead of leather.

Rooney scrambled to her feet, crouching low, and peeked out through the branches.

"I'll take Nightshade," Bridget said, referring to the wealthy seaside avenue at the edge of Warybone where she was sure to earn the greatest sum of moonstones. "You two head to Cold Spine." Colin and Sim stopped messing around long enough to acknowledge their assignment—a lane at the edge of town where no one with any sense would go alone, for even the roughhouse boys might get roughed up there.

Rooney found herself leaning ever so slowly forward, brushing against the prickly bushes, as she waited to hear where Bridget would send Trick. She needed to catch him alone.

"Blackthorn," Trick said before Bridget could direct him, naming Rooney's favorite street with the lovely line of rowan trees along the boulevard.

Of course he'd choose that place, first stealing her mirror and now trying to claim her territory. She almost leaped out at him right then, but she forced herself still and silent.

All the boys went their separate ways, none the wiser that Trick was about to gain a shadow.

With the Monty beside her and a smile spread across her dirt-smudged face, Rooney slunk along, keeping to the darkest patches of the night. At the corner, when Trick went straight, Rooney turned right, cutting through the little park that would take her to Blackthorn even faster. The night he'd stolen her mirror, he'd gone ahead, arriving at the alleyway before her. Well, she could do the same, planting herself right in Trick's path.

Oh, he'd *hate* that she'd turned his trick against him.

When she reached Blackthorn, all was quiet. Rooney and the Monty stalked forward, toward the widest rowan along the boulevard, and tucked into the shadows behind it.

And then they waited.

Not once did Rooney peek around the thick trunk of the tree. Not once did she look down the street for Trick. She didn't have to. Soon enough, she *heard* him. His boots smacking on the cobblestones, his fists rapping against each door as he offered up the moonlight to potential buyers.

Closer and closer he came.

Louder and louder he pounded . . . as did Rooney's heart.

When at last Trick strode into view, the sweep of his long,

dark hair hung in his eyes so Rooney couldn't tell where he gazed. She pressed against the bark of the rowan. She held her breath. One more house, then he'd be past her, and she could pounce.

No one came to the door when he knocked (neither the first nor the second or third times), and Rooney smiled smugly as he stepped back from the stoop.

At the same time, she darted forward. Her hand stretched out. Her fingertips brushed the collar of his coat.

He twisted away, casting a sharp look over his shoulder. Then he grinned, a devilish curl of his lips.

Rooney lunged for him.

Although she was lighter on her feet, Trick was faster. He dodged away, laughing.

"It isn't a game," she huffed, charging for him again. "Give me back my mirror!"

"It *is* a game." Still, he remained out of her reach.

"I'll best you yet, Trick Aidan."

"You can try, Rooney de Barra!" he cried, and then darted down the street.

She bolted after him, legs pumping fast, arms held tight to her sides. The Monty scurried along beside her. Its tongue lolled out of its mouth.

Trick veered away from the dark heart of Warybone, leading her back toward the roughhouse boys. Leading her back toward Thistle Hill.

Didn't matter where he went, she'd follow. Even there,

where the cold, cold patch of air had touched her, where poor Devin Hayes had gone missing.

Somewhere along the way, Rooney had lost the Monty too. It might have run ahead or fallen behind—she didn't know, and she couldn't stop to look for it. Trick was so close now, she could hear the ragged exhalations of his breath. Almost, she could feel the vibrations of his boots clomping over the cobblestones.

Ahead, the air grew dense and hazy, and through it, the Tower of Thistle split the sky. Caught in its cold shadow, Rooney stumbled. Never did she stop, but in that stutter of her steps, Trick gained his lead. It spurred him even faster.

He looked back one last time, that wicked grin cracking his face, and yelled, "Give up now!"

"I'll give up *never!*" she shouted back.

But he turned abruptly into an alleyway, and Rooney lost sight and sound of him.

7

SHROUDED IN SILENCE

The emptiness of the night surrounded Rooney, all at once absent of Trick. The cold had come, and the thinnest fog too. It rolled out of the alleyway, much too creepy for her liking.

She crept forward. *Bravely* forward.

Trick probably crouched in the shadows, waiting to jump out at her.

Rooney rounded the corner and faced the darkened alleyway, feet planted firmly, hands on her hips. "Trick Aidan," she called, but the fog seemed to eat the sound of her words.

Trick made no reply. He made no move to scare her.

Impossibly, he wasn't there at all.

But she'd *seen* him turn this way. He had to be here. She ran forward, all the way to the alley's abrupt dead end, and struck the brick wall with her fist. She looked up and down and all around. There was no place he might have hidden.

She saw no crack or crevice, no window or doorway through which he might have passed. She saw no way he might have scaled the walls, no sewer he might have wormed his way into.

The bone-deep chill pressed closer, same as the one she felt when she'd run from Devin Hayes's house. Rooney did not like its icy touch.

Even less did she like the splotch of darkness spilled on the cobblestones before her. Like a spreading pool of blood.

She circled it carefully. She drew in a breath.

The silky-smooth surface rippled.

A hand shot up from the pitch. Fingers clawed at the air, curled and reaching, but when they grasped nothing but air, they disappeared once again.

Heart pounding, Rooney jumped back. Trick. It had to be Trick. Something in the night had stolen him away, had sucked him into this dark, glossy substance on the stones.

She might be next!

Behind her, a whisper cracked the quiet. "Hush."

Rooney spun around. At first, she saw nothing, only the street beyond the alleyway. But when she squinted and focused on the shadows, she realized she was not alone.

There, beside the grime-gray wall, a figure stood swathed in a hooded cloak of fog.

Rooney pressed a hand to her lips, holding in a startled scream.

Slowly, slowly, the figure's hood fell back, revealing a woman with hair as dark and wild as a sky full of ravens.

It whorled around her shoulders. A shiny black ribbon encircled her throat, and Rooney's fingers slipped from her mouth to her neck, tugging at her coat collar, the top button of which suddenly felt much too tight.

Moonlight struck the woman's pale skin. Long scars fell down both cheeks, like lines of rain cutting across glass.

The magician from the Tower of Thistle.

No one had seen her the whole of the year. Rooney had thought the tower abandoned, it had stood so dark and quiet. But the magician must have been there all this time.

Rooney was too frightened to speak as the magician came closer.

"Have you lost your way in the darkness?" The magician cracked a sharp smile. "Have you lost your friend *to* the darkness?"

Though Trick was no friend of Rooney's, she needed to know what had become of him—he still had her mirror. "What have you done?" she said, unable to spark her voice with the fire that stirred in her belly.

"I've quieted him." The magician touched a fingertip to her temple, as if her head ached. "I've shrouded him in silence and gifted him to the darkness." She gestured to the black stain on the ground.

Rooney's eyes swung downward, and before she could stop herself, she thought once more of blood. Of the magician clipping Trick's tongue from his mouth. Of Trick being well and truly silenced.

But no, *no*. It couldn't be that. The splotch of darkness had corners. It had depth. Like a pocket of night torn free from the sky. Trick's hand had pushed up through the strange darkness.

And Rooney hadn't taken hold of it. One more thing she could not protect.

Rooney hopped out of the way, the moonlit fire inside her burning brighter. "Keep him quiet if you want to"—Rooney did not much care for the sound of Trick's voice either—"but bring him back from wherever you've sent him."

The magician twitched, a contortion of the strange scars on her face.

"I mean it." Rooney found her voice. She raised it loud and clear. "Magic him back!"

The magician's long hair twisted in the wind. "Quiet," she hissed, low in her throat, the ribbon choking each word. "The darkness awaits you."

Rooney backed away slowly, deeper into the dead-ended alley. Her heel dipped into the pitch, sank into it, felt the tug and pull of it. As if she trembled at the edge of a cliff, and below her swirled the void.

What's down there?

She wheeled away, skirting around the darkness as the magician stalked closer. Rooney bent her arms. She readied her elbows, which were the sharpest points on her body. If she got in one good swing, with only a few steps she could be free of the alleyway and flee the magician and her dark magic.

But if she ran, she might never see her lunar mirror again. She might never catch another beam of moonlight or the dust from a falling star. (She might never see Trick again either, and though she tried to push the thought away, it left a sick feeling in her belly to abandon him.)

"Magic him back!" Rooney shouted again, her voice wavering in fright.

With one pale hand, the magician reached out, as if she meant to smother Rooney. "I should have silenced you firstly." The magician pulled up her hood. She all but disappeared in the cloak of quiet.

Rooney tensed. She squinted. She tried to keep the magician, who was surely coming closer and closer, in sight.

But though she couldn't see her, Rooney could *feel* her. The cold drifted nearer.

She glanced down at the void in the cobblestones, which looked as much like a silken scarf as it did a vast hollow. She kicked a pebble with her boot. It clicked and clacked over the stones, and bounced right into the center of the darkness, where it was immediately swallowed.

And silenced.

The cold touched Rooney. The magician's breath upon her neck, her icy hand at Rooney's cheek.

Coming to shroud Rooney in silence.

Rooney dodged away. She prepared to run.

But she could not shake loose her thoughts of Trick—that he'd think her a coward. That running would prove how unworthy she was of being a roughhouse boy. If she wanted something, she had to be brave and go after it.

Wrapped in fog, the magician swept closer.

Rooney might not have had any magic of her own, but she knew it was real and true. Her mirror was made of it, and she would be brave. She would not let it go—the only thing that mattered to her.

She closed her eyes. She *wished, wished, wished* upon the stars somewhere above her for a safe landing, to find her mirror.

To show Trick he was wrong about her.

Then, with a determined leap, she plunged into the darkness.

8

INK AND PITCH

Rooney fell and fell and fell, like she was tumbling down an endless well. She feared she'd never reach the bottom. At the same time, she dreaded the prospect of what might await her below. Such as a grave of bones from all the children captured and tossed into the void before her.

She dared one eye open, then the other, but she could see nothing in the gloom. Not her hands, grasping at air. Not her hair, whipping fast at her face. It clung to her—a veil of darkness—as if she were not made of skin and bones but rather of ink and pitch.

A scream crawled up her throat, and she released it. Loud and shrill and lovely, it cracked the night. She hoped it reached all the way to Warybone far above, all the way to the magician's sensitive ears. Rooney yelled until her throat was raw.

Until, at last, she landed.

Her body made a great splash as she sank beneath cold, cold water. Silky and dark and *wrong* feeling, it rushed over her head. Her boots and coat dragged her deeper. She kicked with heavy legs, reaching and pushing and trying to remember which way was up, which down.

After all that screaming, she had no breath left within her. But she swept her arms through the water, at last breaking the surface.

She blinked and spat out water. The blackness surrounded her, so deep and oily she could barely see through it. Half-drowned, she spun in a circle, but she could not orient herself. All she could do was tread water, frozen with the thought that if she swam in any one direction, it would be the wrong direction and she would never reach shore. If, in this strange place, there was even a shore at all.

"Trick!" she called.

The hushed lapping of the water was her only reply. The magician had been true to her word, *shrouding him in silence and gifting him to the darkness.*

Rooney's limbs went weak, but she had to continue treading, no matter what. Maybe Trick had forgotten or had tired. Maybe he bobbed somewhere beside her, all the air gone from his lungs.

But no. She could not think like that.

With a decisive stroke of her arms, she headed that-a-way, swimming faster now, as it occurred to her that anything might lie beneath her in this water-that-did-not-quite-feel-like-water.

Beasts forged from darkness might grab her from below.

She kicked her legs as hard as she could, fleeing all she could not see. Including the tug of the current that strengthened the more she struck against it.

Something crackled in the darkness.

Far off, then closer.

Rooney churned her arms harder still, needles of cold cutting through tights, through coat, through skin. The water swirled around her like clawed fingers catching hold, sharp with the bite of winter.

An impossible undertow sucked at her scissoring legs.

It yanked.

Rooney had no time to pull the thin air into her lungs. She went under, sputtering and breathless.

Panic lanced through her. Her body convulsed.

That crackling sound rippled through the water, louder now that she floundered beneath it. She threw her arms overhead, stretching for the surface.

Her fingers glanced off *ice*. It spread as fast as frost above, sealing her under.

So long without air, Rooney's chest pinched. Her thoughts clouded.

She pressed her hand flat against what was about to become the icy cover to her coffin.

In her near-death stillness, the current let her go. She floated upward. Her cheek touched ice.

And a pocket of air.

She gulped it down. She breathed.

And oh so carefully, she rapped her knuckles against the fragile layer of newly laced ice. Her face once again met air.

With fluttering breaths, she swam forward, ice fracturing to let her body pass. It was slow going, for the moment she kicked too hard, the current twistered beneath her.

The water only remained calm when she remained calm. Outwardly at least. Inside, every part of her trembled with fatigue and fear.

At last, she waded to shore, but the solid ground beneath her feet brought little reassurance. Who knew how carefully she'd have to tread upon it? Or if it too would lash out against her?

Hesitant to take even a single step, Rooney looked up toward the not-sky from which she'd fallen. She could see it no better than she had from the water. Only the same stretch of black. No doorway. No window. No twisting stairway leading out.

No escape.

Panic welled within Rooney once again. How much like a grave it felt here—buried beneath darkness instead of dirt.

She brought her trembling arms protectively around her

middle, only to immediately unwrap them and grope for her shoulder, her cheeks, her hair.

Somehow, she was completely dry.

It was magic, of course, but a strange and sinister sort.

As if that magic wanted to expose more of its secrets, it thinned the dark veil. Bit by bit, her eyes adjusted to the starless, moonless murk. Not by much, but enough so she could see the winding of the black river beside her and the midnight landscape everywhere else.

Rooney's stomach knotted. There was no telling what might be hidden in the folds and shadows.

With cautious steps, she crept forward. So long as the river ran beside her, she had something to track her way. *But to where?*

Rooney tried to remember what else the magician had said in the alleyway and what the stories told of the thing stealing children away in the night. But it was all a jumble in her head. Everything around her was unknown.

So focused on the darkness ahead, Rooney missed what lay right before her. When she stepped down, something smooshed.

Something *squealed*.

Rooney shrieked, spinning away. She looked all around, but of course it was so dark she could barely see the boots on her feet, let alone whatever creature scuttled so low to the ground.

But it must have seen her, for all at once claws scratched at her ankles, scampered over the tops of her boots, and clambered up her holey tights. The little beast clung to her skirt. It raced up the sleeve of her coat.

Everywhere it touched, Rooney's skin crawled. She swatted and poked, but it was too fast. Reaching her shoulder at last, it dug its claws in and went as still as a stone gargoyle.

Rooney's breaths came in great puffs. Slowly, she turned her head to the side.

Two glossy black eyes stared back at her.

9

THE NOT-SKY

Perched on Rooney's shoulder, the creature clicked its sharp little teeth. It hunkered there, with long pointed claws and fur so black it blended with the night. A ribbed tail curled over her shoulder. Its smudged-white nose twitched.

She might have screamed again, if she were Bridget Mullen. But Rooney smiled.

"Monty!" she exclaimed. "How did you find me here?"

Never, *never* had she been so glad to see the sneaky rat, who must have tumbled into the void just as Rooney had. Its whiskers brushed against her cheek, a gentle tickle.

"I didn't hurt you, did I?" It looked all right to her and neither whined nor hissed. "Sorry all the same."

Rooney rambled on, all her nerves frayed. "We've gotten ourselves into a big mess, thanks to Trick Aidan."

She peered through the gloom, hesitant to move forward. But then something winked in the darkness.

"Monty, look." She pointed.

Ahead, a small light flickered, the faintest blue haze. Oh, it was so familiar.

The faraway gleam and glow of lunar light.

"That might be my mirror just ahead, fallen from Trick's pocket."

The rat gazed into the distance, but it probably saw no better than Rooney. It hadn't even had the sense to scramble out of her way.

Rooney patted its head with the pad of one finger. "Be on your guard."

Then she called for Trick once again, baiting him. She liked the idea of him *knowing* she was coming for him—that she was brave and would take back her mirror. (Though her bravery felt a tiny bit false, for her insides were all aquiver at what else might await them in the darkness.) "Trick!"

Trick, Trick, Trick . . .

Her voice bounded back to her, eerie and muffled. Still, Trick offered no response, but the echo of his name taunted her.

The glimmering light brightened by the smallest degree the closer she came to it. When she reached its source, she stopped, looking all around for Trick. There was no sign of him—only the round silver object on the ground.

A lunar mirror.

Rooney dropped to her knees and lifted the case. A soft glow shimmered in her brown eyes like the tiniest stars.

The clasp had sprung open, allowing the light to slip out through a thin crack. She poked at the little catch, hoping it wasn't damaged, and shut the lid. It closed with a click—unbroken.

It closed like a drape swept across the sky—leaving complete darkness.

The pitch rushed at Rooney, surrounding her, reminding her there was no moon. There were no stars above.

Her heart went wild. It was too dark. Completely suffocating.

She scrambled to open the mirror again, pressing down on the latch, which stuck in place. It felt just *off* beneath her thumb.

With a final, forceful push, it popped open.

The faint blue light swept out. It hung like mist in the air.

But Rooney frowned. The thinnest, smallest crack touched the glass.

It set her heart racing—that her mirror might be damaged. But though it had the same thorned stem etched in the silver, it didn't have quite the same weight or wear. She felt for the little groove along the rim that she knew so well for all the times she'd rubbed her thumb against the smooth surface.

She could not find it.

It sank in then. This was not her lunar mirror.

It must have been Trick's.

"Oh no," she whispered, crushed by the discovery.

The mirror sat cold in her palm. She tightened her fingers around it, trying to convince herself it didn't matter so long as she had this glimmer of light.

"He lost it, I guess," she said to the Monty. "So now it's ours, fair and fully. It might not be my true mirror, but"—she sniffed—"it will have to do."

The Monty shifted on her shoulder. Its claws dug through her coat, sharp little pinpricks that seemed to voice the rat's disappointment.

Turning Trick's mirror over and about in her palm, she feared what might have prevented him from retrieving it.

Rooney stood, and the rat wobbled. She swung around and followed the river in reverse for several steps.

But that unwanted sick feeling jabbed at her belly again. A twist. A knot.

It was more than wanting her true mirror or not knowing how to escape the darkness; it was the thought of abandoning Trick (no matter how rotten he was). He might be lost within the river of darkness, gasping his last breaths. He might be smashed somewhere upon the ground, bones all broken and poking through skin.

Rooney slowed. She stopped.

She whirled back around, glaring into the shadows. "Monty, I think we must keep going."

The mirror illuminated the ground beneath her feet,

soft and glossy black. Now that she could see it properly, she realized it was made neither of grass nor dirt. In fact, her footsteps left no mark; they made no sound as she walked upon the ground. No wonder she hadn't heard the Monty's approach and it hadn't heard her.

Around her, everything was strangely quiet. The river didn't gurgle. No birds sang in the night.

She lifted the mirror, shining the light forward. And there, just ahead, black trees rose in the distance, tall, slim silhouettes. They reached toward the not-sky. Crooked branches and twisted trunks. A most forbidding wood.

She could strike out in another direction. But if she knew one thing about Trick, it was that wherever the tallest tree grew, he would either be found climbing its branches or sleeping beneath it.

"To the trees," she said. The words were not for the Monty this time but for herself.

At the edge of the woods, Rooney paused. Jutting up from the ground, the trees loomed leafless and strange. They stretched, thin and overlong, like the finger bones of monstrous giants clawing up from the ground. The skinlike bark gleamed as glossy and black as the earth, as if they were one and the same.

Branches twitched, heavy with round, rough-peeled fruit that resembled rotten, black oranges and smelled of autumn's fallen leaves. Each long limb bloomed with tarnished-silver flowers that fluttered like moths.

And like moths, they tipped their petaled faces toward the light.

The trees too, they angled toward her. So slow, so subtle. A tilting of their highest branches.

Rooney retreated one step and then another.

Within the woods, something shuddered.

A long, exhaled breath. A shivering. It gusted between the trees. Rooney felt it in her bones as much as she heard it sighing in the dark, dark woods.

It could be Trick, injured.

It could be a monster, waiting.

Rooney straightened her shoulders. The Monty pressed close to her cheek.

She'd come this far. She would find her mirror. With a shaky breath, she took one step forward.

A low voice sliced through the quiet. "I wouldn't dare."

10

MOST UNGOOD

ooney shrieked and scrambled back. Her hand shot out, shining moonlight into the trees. It misted blue over the lowest branches and the silver flowers and the rot-black fruit. She tipped the mirror, sweeping the light higher, where it wavered across the not-sky, the treetops, the thick darkness.

Rooney steadied her hand. The moonlit glow caught upon the spiny tree limbs.

And the upside-down boy hanging from them.

"Trick!" she hissed.

He dangled awkwardly by one leg, a slender branch coiled around his ankle. "The tree caught me as I fell. Don't suppose you'd help me down, would you?"

She gaped at him. "Why should I? Why *would* I?" Her fingers circled around the mirror that was not her own. "You stole my mirror."

"That's why you should help me." His dark eyes gleamed. "If you want it back."

Rooney stalked forward until she stood right beneath him. With their heads cocked, he glowered down at her, and she scowled up at him.

"Give it."

"I know better than that." He crossed his arms over his chest, which looked ridiculous with him swinging there upside down, his dark hair standing on end. "You'd just leave me."

"It would serve you right. For thieving my mirror. For leading us *here*." Rooney tore her eyes away from Trick, peering into the woods again. The darkness folded over and around itself. Around them.

"Help me down, Rooney," Trick implored.

"I'll *knock* you down," she said, then rose to her tiptoes, raised one arm, and whacked his shoulder none too gently.

"Hey!" Trick's arms flailed out as his body swung back and forth.

Rooney reached for Trick's dangling arm and gave a great tug. "The minute you're down . . ." Her breath heaved as she yanked and pulled. "You'd better hand over my mirror."

"You're ripping my arm from its socket," he groaned.

"Don't care." All the same, Rooney released her hold on him. No amount of tugging was going to free him.

In fact, the tree only gripped him tighter, looping the branch round and round his leg. Lashing out at Rooney when she shook its trunk. She dodged out of the way, and the tree pulled Trick higher.

Out of Rooney's reach.

"Ahhh!" Trick cried, his voice gone panicky. He threw his arms toward her, but even when she jumped, she couldn't grasp hold.

"Keep still," she said, recalling how the river had yanked her under when she struggled.

But Trick squirmed and kicked.

And the tree *squeezed and squeezed.*

If Rooney didn't do something—and fast—the branch might pinch off his foot.

Only one idea sprang to mind, but it would be risky, as it involved sharp little teeth.

Rooney grinned mischievously at the Monty. "Hurry him down!"

The rat scampered forward, climbing up the tree's twisted trunk and ambling out onto the branch from which Trick hung. Balanced there, the rat bared its teeth and began to gnaw and chew. Oh, the tree didn't like it much, but the Monty was too quick, too nimble, to be swatted or shaken.

In defeat, the branch recoiled like a length of ribbon unraveling. It unknotted itself from Trick's ankle, dropping him to the ground. He landed with a grunt and grimace, flat on his back, eyes trained on the starless not-sky.

Rooney nudged his leg with the toe of her boot.

He sat up slowly. All the blood that had gathered in his

head from hanging upside down must have been rushing to the rest of his body now that he'd been righted. "Everything's spinning."

"Don't. Care." She held out her empty hand. "My mirror is all I want."

Trick climbed unsteadily to his feet. "Haven't got it."

"Turn out your pockets," she said impatiently, tired of his games.

Grumbling, Trick did so, proving (most horribly) that his words were true. "I lost them both. They slipped from my pockets when the magician swept me into the darkness of her scarf."

Rooney's mouth dropped open. She looked at the trees and the river, at the soft ground beneath her feet that she didn't trust. Was everything made from—*manipulated* from—the same material? Were they really inside the magician's magical scarf? It seemed a most ungood place to be.

Trick continued, oblivious to her distraction. "One mirror tumbled that way." He pointed in the direction from which Rooney had come. "The other fell somewhere over there." His eyes scraped the forest.

Rooney stared at the looming trees. "Then that's where I must go."

"Not alone," Trick said, as if she were not only foolish but also helpless. "It's nice, you know, when someone's got your back."

Now he was just rubbing it in—how he had the

roughhouse boys and she had no one. She gestured for the Monty, who scrambled up the length of her body and settled on her shoulder.

"There's something in the woods." Trick trampled over her purposeful silence, his voice low and anxious. "I heard strange sounds. Whispers and eerie music."

Rooney's skin crawled. But that's probably what Trick hoped for. To scare her. She clamped down her rising fear, latching onto the last word he'd said.

Music.

That reminded Rooney of the missing violin-torturing girl, Devin Hayes, who might be lost somewhere in the darkness as well. It wasn't only Rooney's mirror she ought to search for. "Well, I'm going."

Trick squared his jaw. "And so am I."

He eyed the mirror in her hand. The mirror that brimmed with light for now but would eventually dim. Stranding them in complete darkness.

She clutched it all the tighter so he couldn't wrestle it away, then bravely entered the woods.

They passed beneath the trees, which might snatch them up at any moment. But it was *down* Rooney went, for she stumbled.

Books with cracked spines lay scattered in the path.

Steadying herself, she skirted around them, suspicious of their curious placement here in the woods.

As they stole ahead, they spotted other odd objects.

Alongside a pair of bicycles with bent wheel frames, a rag doll sprawled on the ground, one of its button eyes missing. Propped against a tree, a gilded frame rested crooked, empty of its painting or mirror. Skeins of yarn and rolls of ribbons hung knotted from the trees.

"What is all this junk?" Trick asked.

Rooney shook her head. She had no answer. At least not one that she wanted to voice. For speaking aloud a fear was to know it. And just as she and Trick did not belong in the wooded darkness, neither did these broken things.

She bit her lip, trudging on.

Trick walked beside her, his eyes tracking like a hawk's, his footsteps steady and quick. All at once, he ducked beneath a forked tree, startling Rooney enough that she did the same. The Monty toppled from her shoulder.

The rat had come to no harm, but Rooney gasped. Before her, something glinted silver. Her heart leaped, and so did Trick. His arm lashed forward, fingers touching and then closing around the small object on the ground.

He'd found Rooney's mirror. He *had* known where it had fallen.

Oh, she should have left him dangling upside down!

She opened her mouth to demand he return it, but a prickling along her skin kept her silent.

They weren't alone.

Disjointed music filtered through the trees, all fractured

chords, as if the instruments were out of tune or the darkness warped the tinkling notes.

Rooney sneaked a glance at Trick only to find that he was already looking at her, eyes dark in warning. "Dim the light," he said under his breath.

She did not want to. The darkness would swoop in again, and so would her panic.

Trick watched her. She couldn't let him think her weak. Heart thudding as unevenly as the eerie notes of music, she snapped the lunar mirror closed.

But the woods did not go completely black as she'd expected.

A pale, pale light slipped through the trees. Blue tinged and flickering.

It moved closer.

"Be cautious," Trick whispered. His eyes circled wide with alarm.

Around them, a strange melody drifted in the air, and with it came figures fast approaching.

They pranced along in a disorderly line, a half dozen of them. Some raised blue moonlit torches above their heads. Others played a fiddle or a flute, just out of sync with one another. All of them were children even younger than Rooney. The *missing* children, must be. Wide grins stretched across their faces (some pale, some dark), which bore hideous, gray-dark stains.

Rooney cringed at the sight. She hunkered lower to the ground.

Light leaked between the trees, casting shadow upon shadow. The children skipped through it. Moonlight danced cold in their eyes as they twirled and spun among the trees.

They tilted back their heads and sang a most creepy little tune.

Come out, my friends
Come out, my foes
If you're here
No one else knows

Try if you want
To gather moonlight
But it's gone for good
In this ever-dark night

It's death you've found
And we must confess
There's no escaping
The plentiful darkness

Rooney shuddered. *It's death you've found . . .*

She couldn't be dead; she wasn't. Her pulse raced too surely for that to be true. But chills skated over her skin.

The children marched on, sweeping by the very place

where Rooney crouched with Trick and the Monty. The torchlight grazed over their bowed heads. They flinched away from it. But as the children wandered on, the quiet pressed in.

The *darkness* pressed in.

"Come on," Trick said, drawing himself to his feet.

And so, together (or *untogether*, as she thought of it, as they were more enemies than friends), Rooney and Trick sneaked after the dimming light.

11

AS RESTLESS AS GHOSTS

lue torchlight glowed through trees. Rooney, Trick, and the Monty cautiously stole after it, chasing the spooky seesawing of the children's warped song.

Along the dark path, the toys and books, the trinkets and threads grew more and more abundant. Rooney hopped over a woolen glove without its match. Trick stepped around a paint-peeled wooden horse that might have once ridden proudly on a carousel but now stared at them with one vacant eye. Without a second glance, the children skipped past the curious objects that had no place here—frolicking as restless as ghosts.

Rooney shook the spooky thought away. But Trick must have felt the same foreboding of that song.

"If it's *death we've found*," he whispered, "then perhaps that's what—perhaps that's *who*—we're following. Dead spirits."

From its place on Rooney's shoulder, the Monty chittered. Even the rat harbored suspicions.

Rooney's knees locked up. She froze. "Don't say that."

Hearing it aloud only strengthened the idea of it in her mind. That death waited for them around the corner.

Trick paused when she did. "Come on." He glanced over his shoulder, but his features were lost in the darkness, so his words seemed to rise from the pitch when he said, "I would rather creep up on death than have it creep up on me."

Rooney inhaled sharply, but with Trick's eyes upon her and the challenge in his words, she straightened her back and forged on. The children's high singing voices sent a rash of goose bumps up and down her arms.

They slipped through the trees, winding deeper and deeper into the forest—until they stopped all at once at the edge of a shadowed clearing. Moonlit torches cast the space with a foggy glow. The last child in line spun in a gleeful circle as he sang, eyes sweeping the night.

Trick darted behind a tree, and Rooney squeezed in next to him. With their cheeks pressed to the silky bark, they peeked around the trunk.

The children they'd followed bounded through the clearing (which was not clear at all but spotted with the same sort of broken objects they'd encountered in the woods), and joined a scattering of other kids. The song died on their tongues.

Quiet leaked through the trees.

Be cautious.

Rooney held very still, afraid she'd make some small sound and give their hiding place away.

Within the clearing, the children gathered beneath a black tapestry of tented silk. It draped from the not-sky. Or, it was a part of it. Rooney couldn't quite tell where the swath of fabric ended and the not-sky began.

It was like the walls of this place were ever folding inward, pressing downward.

In the very center of the clearing, on a raised platform sheathed in darkness, sat an onyx throne. Like the trees, it was very narrow and very tall. On it perched a girl no older than Rooney herself. She wore a crown of silver on her dark, dark hair, fine boots that laced all the way to her knees, and a dress the shade of coal.

The girl regarded the other children, a frown on her lips, a glint in her eyes.

And then her head snapped up.

Rooney froze, feeling the girl's sharp gaze fall upon her.

"Come out, my friends!" the girl taunted, her voice high and creepy. Then it dipped low. "Come out, my *foes!*"

12

FRIEND OR FOE?

ooney shrank away from the words stolen from the eerie song and spoken so menacingly. Beside her, Trick's hands knotted into fists.

They (and the Monty) had followed quiet and swift, but all the way through the woods, the children must have known they were there. The group of them turned back, grinning.

Rooney did not like all those eyes upon her. Or the strange tremor humming under her toes.

Before they could step forward or slink away, the ground beneath them rippled.

A shifting and sliding. A furious quaking. The earth changing shape.

Trick stomped the ground with his boot, as if he could bully it still. It only heaved more willfully.

The tree quivered too, long branches swaying, tarnished-silver flowers trembling. A vibration ran along Rooney's fingertips, gentle at first, then more forceful. With a great shudder, the tree shook Rooney away from its trunk.

Her arms shot out. They pinwheeled through the air, but she could not find her balance. Not with the ground pulsing like a solid ocean beneath her.

Trick fared no better. A heavy branch swung down and swatted him twice on the shoulder. He wobbled on unsteady feet.

One after the other, Rooney and Trick fell to the still-roiling ground. It bumped and tumbled them along, the Monty flopping about beside them.

They crashed at the base of the throne, limbs (and one tail) overlapping. Clenching the mirror still in her hand and hoping Trick had the good sense to hold hers tight, Rooney swiped her snarly hair out of her face. She looked up, up, up into the pale, drawn face of the girl on the onyx throne.

"Friend or foe?" The girl's eyes cut like daggers as she tilted her chin, ensuring Rooney saw every angle of her face. Black, scraggly veins ran along her jaw. Grayed skin lurked in the severe lines of her collarbone, spreading like mold.

Rooney gulped, her tongue stuck to the roof of her mouth. As she climbed to her feet, the children slipped closer, their shadows stretching long. Some grinned mischievously, the corners of their curving mouths sharp. Others chewed their already ragged lips or stroked the little gray patches spread on their cheeks and the tops of their hands.

She hadn't imagined it earlier; the darkness clung to them.

"Foe or friend?" The girl leaned forward.

At the edge of the clearing, the trees tilted too, their branches spreading like the legs of a spider. They waited for an answer as surely as the girl did.

Trick stood, shaking out his hands as if he might be readying them for fists. He met her fierce stare, then said, rather darkly, "A friend." He sounded not at all convincing.

Rooney thought about elbowing him, but that might not have convinced the girl either. Until she knew the way of things here, Rooney would play along. "A friend," she said firmly.

The girl looked from one of them to the other. "Prove it." Atop her head, the mothlike flowers woven around her silver crown beat their petals like wings.

Rooney frowned. Wasn't it proof enough that they stood there so obediently instead of tearing the girl from the throne and demanding answers about this strange place?

"What did you bring?" One of the rascals sidled closer, the way the Montys shivered through the alleyway, skittish and bold at once. He poked at Trick's coat pocket.

"What did you bring *me*?" the girl on the throne said sharply.

Rooney had nothing to offer this girl. (Not that she

wanted to give her a thing, except maybe a swift kick to the shins.)

Trick glanced down at the Monty, who was circling around their ankles, as if the rat might be offered as a gift.

"That won't do," the girl said.

"Absolutely not," Rooney said at the same time.

The Monty ran its paws across its whiskers, seemingly unaware they discussed its fate.

"But *those* will do nicely." And quick as could be, the girl sprang down from the throne, reached out her arm, and snatched the mirror first from Rooney's hand and then grabbed the other one from Trick's.

"Those aren't yours!" Rooney cried.

The girl flitted to the platform and settled on the throne once again. She dusted her fingers over the etchings, admiring the lovely lunar mirrors.

Trick glared at the girl. "Give them back. Or I'll *take* them back."

"That's not how it works in the plentiful darkness. Not after we've welcomed you so warmly."

More like creepily, Rooney thought.

"But I will forgive you," the girl continued. "You don't yet know the rules."

"We don't even know your *name*," Rooney said, chilled by the slow smile that crawled across the girl's face.

"What is *his* name?" the girl asked instead of disclosing her own.

"Trick Aidan." Rooney's voice came clipped.

"What is *her* name?" The girl nodded her head toward Rooney.

Rooney watched Trick. She waited for him to pretend he didn't know, or to call her Ratty, but all he said was, "Rooney de Barra."

Around them, whispered in the darkness, the other children offered up their names as well. Too many to remember them all.

Sarah O'Brien. Daniel Moore. Anne Riley.

"Devin Hayes."

So she was here! Rooney swung her head toward this last voice, but in the pinched light, she couldn't find the familiar face of the girl from the window. It would have been a welcome sight.

"And I . . ." The girl on the throne raised her voice above all the others, demanding Rooney's attention again. "I am Sorka of the Darkness."

(Maybe Rooney should have introduced herself as *Rooney of the Alleyway*.)

Sorka glanced at the lunar mirrors one last time. Then she tucked them into the pocket of her skirt, making it quite clear she would not be returning them. "Here, there is only one rule you need to know."

Her grin widened. She kicked her legs up over the arm of the throne, lounging back into its silky folds.

"I can do whatever I want, and you must do as I command."

13

ENTRAPMENT

The words jolted through Rooney.

"No way and never!" she cried, unable to hold her tongue. She didn't like this one bit. She would not play along after all.

"That's rotten and ridiculous! No one tells me what to do." Trick narrowed his blackberry eyes, and for once Rooney knew what it was like to have someone stand beside her when facing off against a *foe*. (It was much better than standing alone—even if it was Trick Aidan and they were still decidedly *un*together.)

Sorka's white cheeks flushed pink. She straightened on the throne once more, boots stamping to the ground without making a sound. "I've made this rule for a reason. It's for your own good!"

"It's good for nothing," Trick growled.

Rooney scrambled forward. She'd rip her mirror—and

Trick's too—from Sorka's pocket. In three quick strides, Rooney reached the little platform and leaped up.

Sorka jerked back in her seat, as if no one had ever before approached her so boldly. "How dare you," she hissed.

Rooney wobbled on the landing, and Sorka caught hold of her arm, fingers tight.

Rooney gasped. Not at the sharpness of Sorka's nails—but at those gray-dark stains on Sorka's pale face, which looked all the more dreadful up close. Creeping and crawling along her jaw.

"If you aren't careful. If you don't *listen*"—the lean smile returned to Sorka's lips—"soon you'll be as lovely as the rest of us."

"The darkness can't touch me." But Rooney knew of nothing to stop it from burrowing and seeping into her skin. Except for the lunar mirrors. Their bright glow might hold it back.

Never mind Sorka's strong grip, Rooney scrambled for the tucked-away mirrors.

Sorka screeched. With the sweep of her arm, the platform lost all its sharp corners. "Away with you!"

Rooney's feet slipped on the newly made slope. Released from Sorka's grip, she lurched backward, crashing into Trick, who'd come up behind her. Beneath their boots, the ground rippled once again, sending her and Trick and the Monty sprawling head over heels and claws away from the throne.

And toward the woods.

Rooney and Trick landed in a heap—his elbow jabbing

her stomach, her knee knocking into his jaw. Hurriedly, they untangled themselves and climbed to their feet beneath the looming trees and the too-close darkness.

Oh, Rooney didn't know what was out there, but it must have been better than this rotten girl and these long-faced children. She started for the woods.

"Wait!" Sorka cried, a startled note to the command.

Rooney marched along with the Monty, strangely pleased that Trick walked one stride behind her. None of them looked back.

"You don't know the woods or what's at the edge of the darkness." Sorka's voice followed them, a warning carved into her words. "You need to listen to me. You need to *stay*."

Rooney spun around this time, but only long enough to say, "No chance!" Especially not with this new knowledge— the darkness had edges. And that must mean it had an end. If she reached it, they might find their way out.

Their way home.

"You'd better learn to behave," Sorka called to them, and then she raised her arm, one quick swirl of her finger and a whisper under her breath.

The children hushed when she did so. They huddled in the darkness, watching with bright-dark eyes. Bright, for they pierced so intensely. Dark, for they harbored such secrets.

Shadows swarmed, cutting through the blue-tinged light of the torches. Soft creaks. A featherlike swooshing.

"Watch out!" Trick warned, but too late.

Long, skeletal branches broke through the night as the nearest trees bowed their limbs. They knifed toward Rooney and Trick like a giant's steepled fingers. All claws and sharp points and ill intent.

Trick yanked Rooney's arm, roughly pulling her along as he bounded away from the bent-backed trees. She stumbled after him. But the branches were everywhere. Chasing and piercing and stabbing. They swung like blackened blades, so fast the air shrieked.

The Monty scampered to and fro, dangerously close to their ankles, and it was all Rooney could do not to trample it underfoot. Clutching Trick's elbow for balance, she swept her arm down and scooped up the rat. Its little eyes rolled wild in its head.

They ran in frantic circles. With the branches twitching behind and before them, there was nowhere to hide.

Rooney and Trick stumbled to a stop. She braced herself, pressing her back against his, scared of moving in any one direction and being skewered by a bough.

"Hold tight," he said.

"Keep still," she warned, hoping these were not the last words she would hear or say.

One after another, the branches thrust downward. Black spikes arrowing toward them. They spindled and speared, rooting into the ground.

Entrapping Rooney and Trick.

11

UNRAVELING

The twisted-trunk trees fell still once more, their long limbs stabbing the ground.

Rooney pushed out a breath, which sounded rather like a growl, and threw herself against the black branches. She wedged her arms through the narrow gaps, but no more of her body would fit. And no amount of shaking broke the strange entrapment.

"Let us out of here!" she screamed.

Sorka glowered at them from the throne. "Not yet, I won't. I can't have you running off." And with that, she turned her cheek, dismissing them.

Rooney whipped around, focusing her bubbling fury on Trick, who stood there with his head nearly touching the entwined branches above him. "What an absolute mess! All because of you!"

Trick gazed through the barlike branches, a quieter anger

simmering on the shaded planes of his face. "It's the magician's fault, not mine."

"It's the magician's fault *and* yours," Rooney insisted. "And *hers*."

Sorka had trapped them, and now she ignored them. Apparently, she meant for them to stew in their disobedience.

With a false note of cheerfulness, Sorka called the children closer and tilted a tattered book to the blue glow of the moonlit torches, preparing to read to them. It must have been a terrible tale, Rooney thought, horror filled and dark. One that would give all the children nightmares.

Trick stepped closer to the tree limbs, staring out at the children and their gray-splotched skin. "There's nearly a dozen of them."

Some of the children shot curious looks at Rooney and Trick from where they sat at the base of the throne. Others had eyes only for Sorka and looked up at her almost adoringly. They must have been fearful of disobeying her commands (and landing in a cage of their own), for there was no reason to *like* that awful girl.

"They're all against us." None of them had lifted a finger to help Rooney or Trick.

"We don't know that," he said. "We don't know anything at all."

Rooney slouched, the fire gone out of her. "I know I don't like it here. I know that I want to go home."

Trick rattled the branches, as if he thought himself strong

enough to break through where Rooney could not. "We *all* want to go home."

Rooney bit her lip, touched with a pinch of guilt. Not at Trick's sharp words, but at the realization that these strange children must have longed for the very thing she did.

Their song ran through her head. The promise that there was no escape.

The thought that death lingered, unseen, but near enough to snatch her.

She smothered her spiraling thoughts. There *must* be a way out.

Rooney dropped herself to the ground and folded her legs. The smudgy Monty nudged her knee, then curled up in a corner of the cage.

Trick slouched down across from them, and when Rooney refused to look at him, he broke the awkward silence rather gruffly. "Let's sort this out, okay? Why would the magician bring us all here?"

"To silence us." Rooney cringed, remembering the magician's cold presence. Her scarred cheeks. That raven-wild hair.

"Must be more than that." Trick considered, then said, "Maybe she doesn't like children much."

"Suppose so." Rooney ran her hand across the earth's glossy, black surface. "But how is it even possible we're here? What must this place be made of to hold us all inside?"

"Magic is how we're here. Magic is what it's made of."

Trick mirrored her suspicions. "And the strangest sort of . . . satin?"

"It's silk."

"If you say so. I've never touched anything this fine."

Rooney picked at the patch in her stockings, not knowing how to respond to Trick when he was being so agreeable. It unsettled her. But she spared it little thought as, just then, her finger snagged the holey wool at the knee of her tights, and an idea popped into her head.

"Well, I don't know much about magic, but silk isn't so special. Not really." She reached out her hand, feeling along the nearest of the silken branches.

"Spiderwebs are made of silk, and they're death traps," Trick said quite unhelpfully, drawing closer the song's blunt threat.

Rooney's throat went dry, but she forced her wandering fingers to continue their way over the branches, slow and careful. "Silk is made of threads just like the wool of my stockings. There's bound to be a loose thread, and all we have to do is find it." Her fingers crept along, searching and seeking. "And begin its unraveling."

There was just enough light for Rooney to see Trick's sly grin and his hands sneaking fast to the tree limbs.

As they hunted, Sorka read to the children, her voice too low for the words to reach Rooney's ears. Only a soft murmuring carried through the night.

Until that stopped as well.

Rooney's hand stilled on the branch. From her perch, Sorka tossed the book to the ground where it landed face-down, spine split, pages ruffled. The children scattered.

If she would treat a book in such a horrible manner, Rooney didn't know what Sorka might do if she saw what Rooney and Trick were up to. Make the cage squish smaller. Bury them beneath folds of silk until they could no longer breathe.

Or even break their lunar mirrors.

Rooney gasped just thinking of it.

As if the darkness itself had heard her, the ground rippled and sighed. Rooney tensed, waiting to be flung about once again, but the vibrations were gentle this time.

Beneath the children, the ground transformed—little bedrolls and pillows of the silkiest black unfolded (none for Rooney and Trick).

Sorka cried, "Torchset!"

A word that made no sense at first. Rooney had only a moment to blink in surprise before the dim moonlit torches snuffed out all at once.

Darkness descended. Like sunset happening all at once.

Panic knotted in Rooney's chest once again.

"Good night, my friends." Sorka's voice glided through the pitch. "Good night, my foes."

All was quiet, except . . .

Somewhere in the darkness, a child wept softly.

15

TERRIBLY LOST

Rooney's breaths came fast at the sudden shock of darkness. The blackout pressed against her, as did the muffled cries of the child, who must have missed his parents very much.

Her heart pinched a bit; her resolve hardened.

She slid her fingertips along the cage of branches. The silk was so sleek, so soft. The children probably longed for torchset each night, when they could lay their heads upon the pillows and dream of the world beyond the darkness.

But what good was dreaming? Rooney would tear her way out of the cage, then cut right through the heavy pitch.

Somehow.

If only the branches were not so stubborn!

"The trees are smooth and perfect," she moaned.

"They are smooth . . . ," Trick began, and then paused. He let out a grunt from somewhere above her. He must have risen to his feet, searching the highest part of the cage that Rooney could not reach. ". . . and *im*perfect."

Rooney jumped up beside him, so close she could feel his breath on her cheek. "A thread?"

Trick did not respond. For many minutes, he fussed with the branches over their heads. Then his hand grazed her own, and he passed her the thinnest, the finest, the most wonderful of threads.

Rooney plucked it gently, feeling it tug away from the branch and unravel. She gathered the length of it in her hands as she pulled and unwound, until so much had come undone that it overflowed from her arms in a tangle.

"Monty. Where have you gotten to?" The rat followed her voice, bumping its wet-and-whiskered nose against her hand. "I need you to do some unraveling."

The Monty took the thread in its mouth and slipped away.

Rooney touched the thinning branch, felt it getting slimmer and slimmer the farther the Monty traveled. "Get ready," she said to Trick, for at any moment there would be just enough space to squeeze through, and they needed to do so before the thread raveled back up and snapped closed the cage once again.

At last, the branch whittled down, wispy as a spider's thread, and Rooney shoved it to the side. She found Trick in the dark and closed her hand around his own. He tensed at her touch, but when he did not shake her off, she dipped through the narrow opening with Trick staggering out behind her.

"Monty," she whispered, but the rat did not come even when she called it a second time.

They took several quick steps before Rooney realized she didn't know where she was going—if she wandered toward the woods or the clearing. But Trick strode confidently ahead, and soon enough, Rooney's eyes began to adjust to the dim, enough so she could just make out the silver flowers fluttering in the trees.

She shot a look over her shoulder, worried Sorka would sneak up behind them. But the girl must have been dreaming (or more likely *nightmaring*) alongside the children, as she was nowhere to be seen.

Trick cocked his head at the not-sky, but now was not the time to admire the darkness. She pulled her hand from his grasp. "What are you *doing?*"

"Getting us out of here before we're patch-marked like everyone else. Didn't you see the shadows clinging to them?" He scratched his arm, his neck, the tip of his nose, as if he could feel the darkness crawling over his skin.

"Of course I did." Rooney scratched her jaw, her elbow, the top of her head, everywhere that suddenly itched.

"I won't let it touch us. We'll escape before then," Trick said.

Those quiet sobs echoed in Rooney's thoughts. Oh, how she would have liked someone to care for her when she'd felt abandoned—as these children now were. "All of us?" she wondered aloud.

"Who says any of the others are even alive?" he asked.

"They aren't dead. They were *breathing*."

Trick's voice came low and serious as he circled one tree and then another. "Maybe the dead never forget how to breathe."

Rooney shook her head, dark hair rippling like shadows. She had trusted in the rise and fall of their chests. But trembling as she was, she could not find her voice to object.

"If the trees behave, maybe we can climb them all the way out of here." Trick placed a hand to the nearest trunk, ready to scale it right then and there.

Of course that would be his suggestion even after how horribly the trees had treated them.

"They *won't* behave. They'd only fling us back down. We'd splat on the ground." Rooney slapped her palms together. "The children would have to dig holes for our graves."

Trick scowled.

Quite decided, Rooney continued, "We need to reach the edge of the darkness. That girl said it was there, and it must be the way out."

"What must be there?" Trick scoffed. "A door? Just waiting for us to swing it open?"

"Won't know until we see for ourselves." Rooney propped her hands on her hips, all the better to put forth her challenge.

He grinned. "Let's go, then."

"Wait for me," a voice whispered through the darkness.

Rooney's head snapped to the side. She hadn't heard a single footstep. The gloom masked whoever approached.

"Who's there?" Trick hissed.

The dimmest, faintest blue glow sparked and almost immediately sputtered out again. Full darkness, and then it flashed again. Closer this time and holding steady.

It illuminated a girl in the shadows, one who wore a long braid over her shoulder and had brown cheeks, thick eyelashes, and a heart-shaped face. Clutched to her chest, she held the Monty, the unraveled thread dangling from its paws, and a stubby candle, the flame of which wavered blue.

"Your rat was terribly lost," she said, setting the Monty on the ground. It skittered to Rooney's side. "But aren't we all?"

Rooney gathered the Monty in her arms, never once lowering her eyes, worried the tiny moonlit wick would blink out again and she'd lose sight of this girl.

"The girl with the violin," Rooney said. "Devin Hayes."

"A violin?" Trick looked keenly at Devin, sizing her up.

"Well, I don't have it anymore. It's gone, just like your mirrors. But I don't care about that. All I want is to go home." Devin ducked her head, wiping her eyes before lifting her chin again. "There's nothing here but darkness and that awful girl on the throne."

Rooney frowned. "I bet she was the first one snatched away by the magician."

"Must be," Trick said, "the way she lords over everything."

Devin ran the end of her braid through her fingers. "Just imagine being here alone. All this darkness . . ." Her shoulders rounded. "It seemed to . . . I don't know . . . *cinch in* when you arrived."

Rooney felt a little dizzy at the thought, like a hand was pressing over her nose, like the sky was falling. The space around her was unknown, unpredictable.

And so was Sorka.

Rooney turned to the woods. "Then let's get going before Sorka—"

Devin's brown eyes widened, her gaze flicking away. "Oh, don't say it. Don't say her name."

But it was too late. It had already escaped Rooney's lips.

The trees shook. The silver flowers trembled. Devin blew out the candle.

Then, like wind through branches, came Sorka's low voice.

"If you say my name, I'll hear it. The darkness will carry your words right to my ear. Even if you whisper."

THE MAGICIAN—
A QUIET NAME

The magician once had a perfectly ordinary name. Firstly, a first name, and lastly, a last name. It had been made of rounded letters and smooth sounds. A quiet name. One that suited her so perfectly. But no one spoke it anymore, and she'd all but forgotten it.

She'd been so careless, misplacing it in the foggy corners of her mind. For when she brought the quiet, when she took the children, tiny bits of herself fell away, stolen by grief. Her name, gone most days. Her heart, gone far longer.

The hollow inside her was all she had left. And how strange it was to be filled with nothing and to have it take up so much space.

The magician pushed herself away from the desk and returned to the gray-glass mirror. Not a hair, not an eye, not the sharp line of her jaw reflected on its surface. She clutched the pocket scarf to her chest, right over the spot where her lost heart echoed.

How dare it still beat, she thought.

A sliver of moonlight lanced between the tower's shutters, catching the edge of the mirror's gilded frame. The moonlight was noisy. Too bright, and therefore too bold. She winced at what she once had loved.

Now she longed only for darkness. The mirror reflected it, and the woods on the other side of the glass. Pitch black and empty but for the trees thick with magic.

The magician peered through the darkness—at the beauty of what she'd created. She stroked her silk scarf, and in the glass, the treetops swayed, as if she'd run her fingers through their branches.

Here, they seemed to say. *This way, this way.*

It was the appointed hour, when the stolen children would be sleeping and quiet. The magician leaned forward. She blew out a breath and whispered a name. "Come. My devil, my dear." The words clouded the mirror before sinking through and past the thin border, from one spinning world to another.

But as had passed the last three nights, the darkness did not answer. The magician had waited. She'd been patient. She'd been careful.

It would not do much longer—this worry eating away at her.

She stayed there all night, half-asleep on her feet. Waiting and waiting.

To remember her name. To hear it whispered in her ear by someone who still knew it.

Tonight, though she was patient, it would not be, and only when dawn broke did she turn her back on the mirror. Did she fall into bed and find darkness in sleep.

16

THE DOOR AT THE EDGE OF THE WOODS

No one made a sound in the darkness. All the same, Rooney knew Sorka approached. Her voice had been so near.

Rooney crouched as small as she could, Devin and Trick stooped beside her, when out of the shadows a flare of blue light speared through the trees. Sorka crept forward, feet bare, ankles spotted gray, her face as rumpled as her dress. In her hand, a lunar mirror shone.

Its pale light flickered in time with the sinister sway of her voice pitching high and low. "You're not where you're supposed to be."

The Monty, all curled up in Rooney's arms, trembled. Rooney tucked closer to the tree before her as Sorka's eyes pierced the night.

"Come out!" Sorka cried, her words twisting cold and sharp. "If you know what's good for you!"

Devin clutched at Trick's arm, and Rooney pressed her lips tight. Huddled all together, they moved not a muscle, not even a hair.

A small murmur gusted through the night, and Sorka swung toward it, taking the glow of the light with her. She slipped through the trees, her slim figure outlined in blue. One step and then another, she moved away from them.

And then she stopped.

Her body bent forward. Her hand reached toward the ground.

Rooney leaned around the trunk of the tree as far as she dared, but she could not see what had captured Sorka's attention—and what she so slowly lifted.

All at once, the Monty squirmed, its little legs scrambling. Rooney patted it. She tried to calm it and quiet it.

Sorka straightened, spine snapping into place. Her head cut to the side, and upon her face a lean smile spread.

The Monty jolted in Rooney's hands. Trick and Devin cast horrified looks in her direction—Devin all squinty, anticipating being found out, no doubt, and Trick, dark eyes slashing, warning her to keep the rat still.

A slow step drew Sorka closer. She hadn't spotted them yet, but soon she would. Her hand touched the air, *tugged* the air.

But that couldn't be. She only had control of the fabric of the darkness, didn't she?

Again, the Monty jerked, so suddenly Rooney almost lost

hold of it. And that's when she noticed the wisp of thread still clasped in its little paws.

The thread that Sorka was tugging. The thread that was growing taut.

That's what Sorka had found on the ground, and now the tangled strand led her toward them. Even if the Monty dropped it then and there, she'd be upon them in moments.

Another yank from Sorka, and the Monty leaped from Rooney's grip. Whiskers twitching, it glanced up at her and Trick and Devin, all of them blinking helplessly. Then it dashed off into the darkness, the thread clenched in its teeth. It ran as if its tail had caught fire, fast, fast, fast away from them.

And Sorka, holding the other end of the unraveled thread, unknowingly chased not Rooney but the rat. Her dark hair streamed behind her as she ran.

When they'd lost sight of her bony form, Rooney, Trick, and Devin hastened in the other direction. They pushed through the trees in the near dark, and only when they reached a safe distance did Rooney whisper, "Oh, Monty."

"What a good friend the rat is to you," Devin said.

"Very," Rooney agreed, which sank her spirits lower, for now she was without the only creature who cared for her. The rat had risked Sorka's wrath, all to keep them from being caught.

"It'll find its way back to us," Trick said, and Rooney could only hope his words proved true.

As they hurried on, Devin lit the candle from a tiny bottle of moonlight, and once she did so, the soft blue light fell upon a scattering of oddments—just as they'd spotted when they'd first entered the woods. Where had this random assortment of objects come from, and *why* were they here?

"How sad it is, all this rubbish," Devin said, sidestepping a fractured teacup.

And it *was* sad. The objects were broken and torn and cracked, every last one of them ruined in some way. Forgotten things.

A little bear with its stuffing unstuffed.

A hairbrush missing its bristles.

A clock with its golden hands stopped at midnight, and a pair of ballet slippers, the pink satin as smudged as the Monty's nose.

Trick's jaw tightened when they passed a disjointed clarinet with a chipped reed and missing keys. "You think all this stuff spilled through the *door* at the edge of the woods?"

"Might have," Rooney said sharply, but her insides quivered.

She'd owned things like this once, and she'd taken much better care. The charm bracelet from her father, dangling with silver stars—it had always circled her wrist so prettily, the charms clinking and tinkling against one another. And the little telescope her mother had given her, small enough to keep in her pocket or tuck under her pillow each night—it had always found a way into her hand as she sneaked from her bed and drew back the curtains so she might gaze at the stars, finding the constellations her parents had shown her.

We gathered the stars for you, Rooney.

Those gifts had meant so much to her. They were the very last things she'd sold when she'd run out of moonstones—and before she'd found her lunar mirror.

It had felt like handing over tiny pieces of her heart. She missed those small trinkets.

But most of all, she missed her parents. Very much. So fiercely.

Had they still been alive, they would have pushed back the darkness and put an end to this nightmare. They would have drawn her safely into their arms. Her lip trembled.

"What is it? What's wrong?" Devin turned, looking all around, as if Sorka might have circled back and sneaked closer through the trees, quiet as a ghost.

"Nothing." Rooney hadn't realized she'd become so lost in her thoughts that she'd fallen behind the others.

"*Everything*, you mean. Can't you see all these broken things?" Trick scowled at her, but his voice softened, as if wary of his own words. "And we're just like them."

Rooney flinched. He shouldn't have said that. He didn't know a thing about her. "I most certainly am *not*."

Yet she could not help but think he was exactly right. Her heart was a shattered thing, and there was no repairing it. She wondered what bits of Trick lay wrecked inside. It was hard to believe he felt that way.

His dark eyes soured and shuttered at her stern denial. "Come on, then. There's no time to waste."

The three of them charged forward, Rooney overtaking Devin, then Trick. They ran past fallen toys and trinkets, until the trees began to thin and they left the heart of the woods behind.

Until they found a black cobbled road, all broken to bits, stretching out before them.

17

THE MOST WICKED

Rooney stumbled over the jagged cobbles, but she did not slow. This road of rubble and stone, as dark and winding as the silken river, must lead somewhere.

Maybe to the edge of the darkness.

"Hurry," Rooney called, for there was no telling when Sorka would catch on to the Monty's little trick. And if there was a way out (a door or otherwise), they needed to reach it before it was too late.

"Careful," Trick said, and Rooney tossed an anxious look back just as he clasped a steadying hand on Devin's arm.

The light from the candle jumped all about as Devin staggered along. Its blue glow bounced off their faces, casting strange shadows that reminded Rooney of the darkness crawling across the children's skin.

"Come on!"

But Trick and Devin suddenly faltered to a stop.

Their heads tilted back. They looked up and over Rooney's shoulder. Devin raised the candlelight.

Hairs sprang up on Rooney's arms. She spun around.

A dark tower stood at the side of the crooked road. It leaned toward them, gray stones misaligned and crumbling, the roof cracked, its door hanging open from greasy hinges. In the quiet, a grating sort of sound shivered through the air—stones shifting ever so slowly out of place.

"The Tower of Thistle," Devin whispered, as though she feared the magician would descend the spiral stairway and storm out to punish them.

Rooney backed up, clunking into Devin and Trick. Her eyes raked the night, but everything remained still. No one sneaked out of the decrepit tower or peered down from the high windows.

"It's only made to look like the Tower of Thistle," Trick said. "But it can't be. We're not in Warybone."

"Not *yet*," Rooney said, and edged forward, pulling Devin along with her so the light shone ahead.

They crept over the coal-black cobbles, giving a wide berth to the tower, which threatened to collapse upon them should they disturb it.

"What happened here?" Devin's voice shook, as did her hand.

Rooney held her breath as they passed the tower, tripping over the loose cobblestones, then breathed out. "I don't understand a thing about this place."

"It's like a warped mirror of the world above," Trick said.

If that was true, Rooney did not much like this bleak reflection: the stream now as wide as a river and deathly cold; the wilder lands grown thick as a forest; the familiar streets of Warybone narrowed to one frayed ribbon edged with a straggle of broken lampposts and trees.

And the not-sky, eating the light.

The candle still glowed in Devin's hand, but its radius of moonlight grew smaller and smaller. Rooney could no longer make out the buckled road ahead.

Because there was no road ahead.

It ended abruptly in a scattering of broken stones. Rooney, Trick, and Devin froze.

Before them rose a wall—of darkness. So thick, so plentiful, it swallowed the candle's light. When Rooney squinted and focused and stared very hard, she could see that the rippling wall extended on and on, and up and up, until it disappeared in shadows too far and too dark for her to glimpse the end.

"The edge of the darkness," Rooney whispered.

"What . . ." Devin cleared her throat. "Whatever was at the end of this road is *gone*. Like it was *sucked up* by the darkness."

Rooney put on a brave face. "Or else it's just beyond reach."

Tentatively, she stretched out her arm.

"Oh, *don't*," Devin said in a small voice.

But Rooney had to, and so she let her fingers dip into the

inkiness, touching nothing and nothing and more nothing. As if she'd reached into a space that didn't truly exist. Her hand all but disappeared in the pitch, then her wrist and her elbow followed. Cold seeped into her skin.

She thrust her arm deeper, until her fingertips brushed against something soft and silky, like woven threads. Except they were just as *not-right* feeling as everything else here.

They slithered.

She cringed away, not wanting to become ensnared in the coils of darkness.

Trick grinned bitterly, his blackberry eyes like pits. "It's a dead end, not a doorway."

Rooney bristled at the way his words stung. "We just have to . . . open it."

Boldly, she reached out again. Her hand groped, first to one side, then to the other, but no matter where she touched, she found the same thing. A pitch-black wall that felt like a threadbare web.

It creeped over her skin, so cold, so spidery.

With a determined grunt, she tore her hand through the darkness, shredding its first frail layer. An icy rush of air gusted against her face. The brittle scent of autumn leaves spilled from the gash.

"It almost smells like home!" Devin exclaimed.

Rooney shot a smug look at Trick. "Guess we have to make our *own* door. One that will drop us right back into Warybone."

Trick spun around, scanning all the broken things strewn beside the cobblestones, then stalked from one discarded object to another. He flung things this way and that, careless for where they landed, and gathered three items up in his arms.

A rusty-tipped letter opener.

A silver butter knife.

A useless pair of scissors with only one blade.

The metal flashed in the dim as Trick offered them up. Rooney grinned, snatching the letter opener because it looked the most wicked. She touched her finger to the tip. Though rust crackled along its surface, the point was very sharp and stabby.

Devin took hold of the dull knife, leaving Trick with the single-bladed scissors. They approached the wall of darkness, Devin to Rooney's left, Trick to her right.

It seemed a strange thing, to be standing so close to them. For once, Rooney wasn't alone.

Trick raised the halved scissors above his head, then quickly thrust down, jabbing the tool into the darkness.

The point sank beneath the surface, and from the depths came a great hiss. Rooney jumped, but Trick held steady. He drew his arm left to right, pulling the blade as fast and fierce as he was used to swinging his fists. Maybe to him, this was only another kind of brawl.

Rooney and Devin threw their arms out at the same time. They plunged the letter opener and the dull knife into the wall, as if they held the sharpest of daggers, and the darkness would yield to them.

The weave unraveled where they cut. It curled like smoke.

Cold, cold air lanced across their faces, spiraling out from the fissures. It rushed wildly around them. It *tugged*. The ends of Rooney's long hair whipped forward, Devin's braid too. Their skirts flapped around their legs, pulled by an invisible force. The candle flew from Devin's hand, sucked right into the darkness.

"No!" she shrieked as the last pinprick of light snuffed out.

The scent coming from the hole deepened and darkened, no longer reminding Rooney of dry, just-fallen leaves. She covered her nose, but the smell—like something burnt to ash, like something *rotten*—curled up her nostrils.

Devin backed away, gagging at the stench, but Rooney hacked again at the wall. She could feel that wispy layer thinning.

Black fog churned, it *bled*, from the places they carved into. Thicker and thicker, it gathered, sliding around their wrists and their ankles, around their waists and their throats.

Devin dropped the knife, which immediately spun away into the darkness, and waved her arms to ward off the fog. Trick slashed at the air, his blade passing right through it.

As Rooney continued to jab at the webbed wall, she struck something solid. *Something living*, she could not help but think.

It let out a great shriek.

The silver letter opener dropped from her hand, gobbled up by the darkness as Devin's knife had been.

They stumbled away as the webbing tore like a wound ripping open.

Beyond, a black hole spun.

A wave of dizziness fevered through Rooney. She stared, hypnotized by its rotation, by its heartbeat of curves and swells.

Such a cold energy spiked from its center, vibrating in her chest and in her limbs. It pulsed before them. It pulled, like a tornado lashing her closer to the center of its vortex. She struggled against it, digging in her heels, and so did Devin and Trick.

But their toes lifted from the ground. Their bodies twisted in the air. The gravitational force yanked them toward the black hole.

A doorway to death.

"Fight against it!" Rooney cried, arms thrashing, while Devin tossed herself all about.

Trick flipped upside down. His arm stretched long; his boots pointed to the not-sky. With a great howl, he stabbed his one-bladed scissors into the ground beneath them, lodging it there among the cobblestones—keeping himself from the maw of the void.

"Grab my ankle!" he shouted, words muffled by the fog that continued to circle.

Rooney swung her arm around, hooking her fingers on Trick's frayed pants. With the additional weight, the scissors slid through the silken ground, dragging them nearer to the black hole.

Her stomach lurched as fog plumed from the cut. Trick's blade juddered, then caught hold, wedged between two crooked stones.

Devin's fingers curled toward Trick's other leg, but the void wrenched her out of reach. She tumbled through the air, her eyes flashing all around—finally landing on the swirling black hole that awaited her.

Devin screamed.

"Grasp on to that tree!" Rooney yelled.

Devin spun around. Her fingers grazed the end of a branch but lost hold.

"The trunk's wiggling like a loose tooth. Kick its branches toward her!" Trick groaned, fighting against the pull of the void.

Rooney flung out her leg. Her heel cracked against the tree. It leaned farther to the side, and whatever planted it in the ground snapped as would roots. The trunk tore free. Branches smacked against Rooney's thigh, sending her and Trick flying after Devin.

All three of them crashed toward the churning pitch, the tree alongside them. End over end, it spiked through the air, falling across the black hole and snarling in the weave of darkness.

Their bodies struck the tree. They threw their arms around the trunk and, all in a row, hung on for dear life.

The black hole swirled just before their noses. Gravity clawed at their airborne legs.

One after another, the forgotten objects flew past their faces. Some caught in the fog. Some slipped through it, disappearing forever.

Rooney thought her hair would be pulled from her scalp. That her skin would be dragged from her bones. She tightened her grip on the tree and screamed, but even that shrill sound was stolen by the void.

All the while, the fog, the *magic*, circled Rooney, Trick, and Devin. It coated their hair, their eyelashes, their skin. In and out it went with each of their fast breaths. It filled their lungs until Rooney could scarcely breathe.

"Oh no," she coughed out, catching one last clouded-gray glimpse of Devin and Trick.

And then she could say and see no more, for she fell unconscious.

18

A LIVING GRAVEYARD

Rooney woke groggy. Her thoughts spun, or it might have been the black hole tossing her round and round.

Except her body wasn't moving. Not even a bit.

But something scuttled through the darkness. It drew closer. Tiny claws plucked at her hair.

She lay on her side, cheek to the ground, so when she cracked open her eyes, all the world grew atilt: fallen trees; the overlap and sprawl of Trick's and Devin's legs; the single-bladed scissors.

And a rat nosing up to her face.

"Oh, Monty," she whispered, sitting up slowly for all the bruises she'd suffered.

Rooney put a hand to her head, out of sorts. The fog that had seethed from the wall still clogged her brain.

And all the fear that had flooded her chest still overflowed there, unshakable.

Before her, in the very spot she'd stabbed the letter opener, the dark hole pulsed. Like a rotten heart beating behind a rib cage made of twisted darkness. Mistrustful, she scooted away, worried the fog would rise again and the hole would yank her forward, not finished with her just yet.

Rooney whipped toward Trick and Devin. They lay on the ground so still and quiet, as if they might never wake. As if the darkness might have stolen their breaths.

"Devin?" Rooney said. "Trick?"

A groggy groan broke from Trick's throat. His fingers twitched. Devin rolled from her back to her side, her braid falling across her chin. Rooney crawled over, more relieved than she could say, and shook them awake.

"Enough, Bridget," Trick mumbled, shrugging off Rooney's hand.

"Mother?" Devin's long lashes fluttered, and she opened her eyes.

Rooney sat back. She brought her knees to her chest and wrapped her arms tight around them. "It's just me." Not at all the person they each had hoped it might be.

A great disappointment sat heavy inside her—that she had not succeeded in gouging a hole back to the starlit streets of Warybone. She hung her head. She'd almost gotten all of them killed.

"I thought we were done for," Devin said, sitting up and

warily looking at the wall. So slowly, the darkness continued to weave itself thicker and deeper, building a barrier between them and the black hole.

Trick pushed his hair out of his eyes. "At least it didn't hurt us any."

But in that instant, his pale face exposed, Rooney feared he was wrong.

She squeezed her bent legs, keeping her hands from trembling. She stared and stared at Trick and then dared a closer inspection of Devin. Without a light, it was harder to see but not impossible.

Specks of darkness clung to them.

A small patch of it lay across Trick's temple. A splotch of gray marked the slender curve of Devin's neck.

"The darkness." Rooney swallowed. "It's touched you both. There and there." She pointed.

Devin's frantic hands flew to her neck. Trick scraped his fingers across his forehead.

"It's not budging," Devin said, but that didn't stop her from scratching the smudge on her neck. Her nails left tracks on her skin.

"Where has it touched me?" Rooney didn't want to know, not really. But *not* knowing was even worse.

She thought it might tingle, a cold, dead spot clinging to her, but she was chilled all over, no part of her shivering more than any other. She shoved up the sleeves of her coat, twisting her forearms so she could see every angle.

"Hold still." Devin brought her braid from her right shoulder to her left, covering the side of her neck where the darkness crouched. She set a hand on Rooney's boot, steadying her, and then looked her over, toes to head.

Rooney knew the moment Devin spotted the gray-dark upon her. A little gasp escaped from between her lips.

"Tell me."

Leaning forward, Devin touched Rooney's cheekbone. "Here."

The darkness had settled on the place where her mother had once laid good-night kisses.

Rooney traced her fingers over her cheek. The surface of her skin was smooth. The darkness had well and truly become a part of her.

Trick, who had been so quiet, looked at them gravely. "It's death," he said. "Coming for us slowly."

"No, no, no," Devin cried.

Around them, the darkness shuddered like an aftershock, and in that moment Rooney knew the cinching-in feeling Devin had spoken of, for the space around them felt ominously closer, like the walls of the not-sky would envelop them.

When they struck into the silk, the darkness had not only woven itself tighter—it had most decidedly *shrunk*.

"Come on," Trick said, rounding them up. "It's not safe here."

Neither Rooney nor Devin asked where they were going.

They only climbed to their feet, frowns drooping from their faces. No one looked at one another. No one said a word. Very much untogether and apart, they wandered through the trees until they spied the frail blue light from the clearing. They followed it forward . . . for they had nowhere else to go.

~

From the throne, Sorka and the children around her watched Rooney, Trick, Devin, and the Monty return. Sorka must have seen the defeat and the fear hanging from their long faces. She must have seen the gray patches newly latched onto their skin. Yet she did not gloat or smirk as Rooney might have expected.

Sorka's eyes brewed a storm.

"How did you escape the cage? What magic did you call?" She spiked to her feet, looming over them, tall and willowy and grave, a black ribbon in her hair replacing her crown. "Are you apprenticing? For *her*?" Sorka's tone was full of accusation.

Rooney had no idea what Sorka was talking about. And more, she did not like the way Sorka stared down her nose at them. "None of that matters! Look what's happened to us!"

"And whose fault is that? I told you to behave, but you threatened the darkness. Doubt you'll do that again, will you?" With her near-black hair and her dress of coal, Sorka blended in with the pitch, and right then her silly title *of the Darkness* seemed much less silly and all the more fitting.

"We only want to return to Warybone." Trick took a step forward, unafraid. "Don't you?"

Sorka's eyes shuttered. Her voice lowered, as if she did not want the children to overhear. "This realm is wholly dark and impenetrable. Like a living graveyard. And there is no digging your way out of it."

Rooney shuddered. They'd found that out well enough, the black hole like a crypt. "Yes, and . . ."

Sorka rattled on. "It can't be burnt or torn. It can't be sliced or cut. You cannot gouge a hole into its flesh." Sorka seemed to delight in every harsh word. How each proclamation made Rooney and Devin flinch. "And it can be very temperamental."

"You tried to warn us," Devin said softly.

Sorka's jaw clacked shut. She'd probably expected more argument, and Rooney was brimming with all the things she wanted to say—to *scream*—but she bit her lip.

"I didn't want any of this to happen." If Sorka meant it as an apology, it was a lousy one, Rooney thought. Sorka might have been talking of the cage of branches, the gray creeping over their skin, or the whole of the darkness pressing in on them.

"But you didn't stop it," Trick said, his voice bruised all over. "And now we're doomed."

One of the children—the boy who'd poked at Trick's pocket—began to cry.

With a final glare piercing Trick, Sorka reached for the

crying boy. She patted the top of his messy-haired head. "Let's play a game," she said, and turned abruptly toward the children so anxiously looking up at her.

And so, left alone, Rooney, Trick, and Devin passed the night lost in their own thoughts, too gloomy to utter more than a few spare words to one another.

Rooney could not even be bothered to devise a plan to steal back her mirror. What was the point? What was the need? She'd never gather moonlight again if she were to die here.

19

THE WHISPERS
IN THE WOODS

Rooney's growling stomach woke her the next day (or at least what she assumed was the next day, evidenced by the torchlight). She'd imagined many tragic ends for them, but she hadn't before considered that they might *starve* to death.

"Hungry?" Devin sank down beside Rooney, gripping her bunched-up skirt like she held something within it.

"Deathly hungry," Trick said from where he lay on the ground, his jacket tucked in a lump under his head.

Devin reached into the cradle of her skirt, then held out her hand. Trick sat up, his shirt all rumpled, and accepted one of the black-rinded fruits.

"What is it?" He peeled back the rotten-looking skin, revealing purplish wedges.

Devin shrugged her slim shoulders. "They called it a grimace fruit."

"How does it taste?" Rooney asked, no doubt the more important question, especially with a name like that.

"Not bad." Devin peeled one and passed it to Rooney. "It's only the appearance that makes you grimace."

Rooney separated a fruit wedge, which was strung with pith as gray as a cobweb, and hesitantly placed it on her tongue. She bit down. It tasted sweet.

But though the fruit filled her belly, it made Rooney's mood no better.

However, Rooney thought, the one in the foulest of moods might have been Sorka. "What's *she* got to be so glum about?"

Trick and Devin swung their heads to the side.

Some of the children—in frilly skirts, overlarge jackets, and hats too broad for their heads—acted out a play in front of the onyx throne. Instead of giving the children her attention, Sorka frowned, her eyes looking past them into the woods.

"She has the best of it, but she acts like a sullen queen of the darkness." Rooney ignored the fact that having the best of something terrible wasn't worth much. "She takes what she wants. She does what she wants. And she's just as miserable as the rest of us."

"Well," Devin said thoughtfully, and began fiddling with the hem of her skirt, as if to keep her hands busy and away from the stain of gray on her neck. "You can have something someone thinks you want, or thinks you ought to have—just as I had the lovely violin my parents gifted me—but that doesn't mean it was what I wanted."

"Or what you needed." The words fell heavy from Trick's mouth.

Rooney looked at him in disbelief—how solemnly he spoke, without an ounce of mocking in his voice.

"Well, I don't feel sorry for her at all," Rooney said. "Even if she's been here longer than anyone."

But as soon as she said it, that dreaded sick feeling stirred in her belly. *How long* had *Sorka been lost in the gloom?*

❧

That night, Rooney slept fitfully with these thoughts, all twisted up in dreams of darkness. And so, when she opened her eyes to the pitch, it was no different from when they were shut, and almost, she could not tell wakefulness from slumber.

I must *be awake*, she thought, *for the cold is in my bones.* Her teeth were near chattering.

Huddled in her coat, Rooney curled into a ball, trying to warm herself, trying to drift back to sleep. She shivered and listened to the night.

Within it, the children breathed heavily. Maybe it was only because of the cold, but something seemed to weigh on the air. It filtered thick through her lungs.

It felt decidedly *not right*.

Or maybe it wasn't the air. Maybe it was the darkness itself.

Those small patches of it graying her skin, and it might have wormed its way into her body too—coiling through her airways, leeching onto her organs, seeping into her blood and bones.

Thoughts running too wild, Rooney bolted upright.

The Monty squeaked at the disruption, dashing out from its place behind her legs, then scampered away.

She squinted into the darkness. All its many folds swallowed the rat right up.

Even with the pinprick speckles of blue light glowing from the woods.

No, glowing from *above* the woods.

Maybe she was dreaming after all, to be seeing something that couldn't possibly be there. She blinked and blinked. The light remained constant, and though it shone so dimly, a moonlit flame ignited in her chest once again.

Rooney leaned over, clumsily shaking Devin's shoulder and then nudging Trick with her stockinged foot. "Keep quiet," she whispered in their ears before they could fuss at her for waking them. "Please. Just look."

In the dim, she couldn't quite see their reactions, of course, but when they were sitting shoulder to shoulder, she felt them shivering beside her.

"It almost looks like . . ." Trick paused, as if he didn't want to say aloud what he hoped for.

What Rooney hoped for too. "It might be; it is."

She stuffed her feet into her boots, tied hasty knots, and

scrambled to stand. Trick and Devin did the same. Careful of the many fingers and toes of the fretfully sleeping children sprawled on the ground around them, they sneaked toward the light.

When they entered the woods, it wavered in and out of view, caught behind the lacework of overhead branches. But there was no mistaking it.

"Moonlight," Rooney sighed.

A narrow beam cascaded down, so pure and frail. It fell as if from a distance even greater than the one between the sky and the earth, and a pocketful of stars glinted faintly.

Rooney could see the soft lines of Devin's face, the wonder in her eyes. They'd all thought the stars were lost forever.

"But how?" A tear glimmered on Devin's eyelashes.

"Maybe your parents tore the sky apart looking for you." Somehow, it was both the kindest and the cruelest thing Trick could have said.

If only it were true.

"No one's found us just yet." Rooney did not mean to be harsh, but it wouldn't do any good to get their hopes up.

"But they might," Devin said, and she dashed ahead, the length of her braid swishing against her back.

"To the light," Rooney said, and she saw the smallest of grins edge across Trick's face.

Rooney and Trick chased after Devin, weaving between the trees and hopping over the toys and trinkets littering the path. They drew closer and closer to the sliver of sky where the darkness thinned.

And where the air thickened.

Only once their hearts settled and their breaths quieted did Rooney hear the whispers in the woods. At first, she thought it must be two or three of the children come to see the stars as they had. But Trick brought one finger to his lips, as if he didn't trust the voices.

Be cautious, he seemed to say.

They stole between the trees, circling closer to the true sky and the murmurs. And then they stopped all at once, Devin's arm swinging out to keep them from going any farther.

Rooney shivered again. No wonder it was so very cold.

Drenched in soft moonlight stood Sorka . . . and the magician.

20

QUITE LOST

Rooney stared and stared. At Sorka. At the magician. At the moonbeam tumbling through the darkness and wrapped around the magician's wrist three times.

She'd never seen light fall in quite this manner, stretched so thin and from such a distance. A few stars, which must have been the very brightest in the sky, blinked above.

And looking up at them, Rooney and Trick and Devin all must have been thinking the same thing—maybe they would learn of a way out of this place. Tucked behind the trees, they tilted their ears toward the secrets.

"Sorka, my devil. Sorka, my dear." The magician's voice came hushed as she traced her fingers along the gray-glass mirror propped against a tree. "When you did not come to the mirror, I feared what had become of you."

"Doubtful." Sorka narrowed her eyes.

"Truthful," the magician replied, her billowing cloak betraying her calm. "Have you lost count of the hour?"

"Yes, and no, and maybe," Sorka said, standing there as if she were the magician's shadow, not a girl. "There is no telling night from day. It is all the same to me."

"All the hours are rushing right by in Warybone, but not here. Not here. Where the darkness holds time near still. Where the quiet keeps you safe."

"Where I can do what I want." Sorka tossed her hair, and a tight little frown cracked across her gray-marked face. "Except there is no longer anything here I want to do."

"Doubtful."

"Truthful." Sorka tilted her head, a low-boiling anger flushing her pale cheeks.

The magician's jaw sharpened. "Yet here you must stay. Where I can always find you."

Sorka cupped her hands around her mouth like she meant to whisper a secret. Rooney leaned forward, not wanting to miss a single word.

"Oh no, I am quite lost, you see. There is no finding me."

"She's talking nonsense," Trick whispered.

But it made sense to Rooney, who felt so lost as well. Stuck in a place no one knew existed. Devin had all but said the same thing when they first arrived.

Again, Rooney considered how long Sorka might have spent in this lightless place. Rooney counted off the past few nights in her head, wondering when she too would lose track of the days entirely. When they would blend and bleed together.

Among the swaying trees, the magician stood stone still, her bones unflinching. "You are where you belong, Sorka."

Sorka winced, as if her name resounded too loudly. "So you've said. So I once thought." Her hand drifted forward, toward the moonlight streaming down like the thinnest piece of lace. "If that's true, won't you stay?"

The magician drew back, the moonbeam shifting with her. "Of all the foolish things to suggest. Even now, it is all I can do to keep the balance here." The air shivered. "I cannot hold back the darkness from within it. And above, the door-way is vulnerable."

"But I want—"

"All this time here, and you haven't learned a thing about it." The magician's voice broke.

One by one, the stars above winked out. The moon-light thinned like a spent breath. As for the magician, her cheekbones sharpened in the darkening night. Cold rolled off her taut body in waves. It inched toward Rooney's toes. She backed up, elbow to elbow with Devin, and Trick across from them, shoulders hunched against the chill.

"I've learned plenty," Sorka said, swirling her fingers through the air.

The ground trembled under their feet, and Devin snatched Rooney's hand. Rooney tensed, but none of them went rolling.

The magician cocked her head. "Is it all a game to you, Sorka? You don't know the firstly thing about magic. Neither its grace and breadth—"

"You've given me no guidance!"

The magician clutched the tenuous moonbeam. "Nor its limits, which I've reached." A look of regret crossed her face. "Too soon."

The ground shook more forcefully, sending tremors up Rooney's legs.

"I must go." With one last searching look at Sorka, the magician lifted her moonlight-curled arm and called to her magic, letting the moonbeam carry her skyward. Up she went, out of reach past the branches, past the treetops. Plunging through the darkness in reverse.

Sorka never once glanced up. She darted into the trees, running farther from the clearing, farther from Rooney and Devin and Trick, who stared after the magician until she had floated out of sight.

"Don't leave us here," Devin said, barely loud enough to be heard.

The thinnest thread of moonlight still wafted down, slanting between the trees where Sorka and the magician had just stood. Devin released Rooney's hand, drawn toward the lovely light. It glimmered; it teased, and Devin reached for the end of the moonbeam, as if she might wrap it three times around her wrist and follow the magician back to Warybone.

Back to her parents, who she must have missed so much.

"Help me." She cast dark eyes at Rooney and Trick. "It's our only chance."

Trick ran forward, and then he bent one knee. Devin set her boot on his thigh, boosting herself higher. She stretched and stretched, trying to gather the fleeting moonbeam in her hands.

But Rooney hesitated. "We can't go now. We can't leave just yet."

"Of course we can. We have to." Trick held Devin's ankles to keep her steady, but he looked right at Rooney when he spoke, his brows drawn together. "We've found our doorway."

Rooney bowed her head, but she wanted to scream again—about that child in the night she heard crying, and all the ones who never cried but hurt no less. Trick would scoff at her. He didn't care about them. He didn't care about anyone but himself and maybe those awful roughhouse boys.

Someone had offered her the magical lunar mirror when she needed it most, and now these children were in need. Rooney could not go without them—not when she knew that black hole spun so dangerously close to them.

She lifted her head. "What about the others? Would you just leave them here to wither and rot in the darkness? Would you throw them to the black hole?" And the Monty too (the Monty *especially*). After all it had done to help her, she could not forget its kindness.

Devin paused with her hand still raised. On Trick's leg, she wobbled and then stumbled to the ground.

"I can't catch it." Forlornly, Devin watched the dwindling moonlight. "But even if I could . . ." She sighed. "It isn't right to leave anyone behind."

Trick climbed to his feet, looking sharply at Rooney. He reached for the moonbeam, so delicate now, almost gone. "We're not wasting this opportunity."

Dismay flooded through Rooney. Just as she'd thought, he didn't care. If he could, he'd return to Warybone without thought or mind of what became of them.

21

THE TRUTH OF IT

Rooney scrunched up her face, twisting her features into the most disapproving, disappointed arrangement she could muster.

All for waste, as Trick wasn't even looking at her. Whereas Devin's hand had passed right through it, his fingers tangled in the moonlight the way weavers crafted it into impermanent string and bows.

A soft melody filtered through the woods. But it was not made by the children with their off-key instruments and high-pitched voices.

Rooney's mouth dropped open.

Somehow, Trick's fingertips strummed the fading light, the notes plinking like rain on a rooftop. Rooney didn't know if the music was magic, exactly, but it sounded like it could be, beautiful and hollow and echoing through the trees. She stared at him in surprise—that his hands, fisted and angry more often than not, could touch the moonlight so gently.

"It's not strong enough to carry us all. I just thought . . ." He glanced at Devin, who looked both fragile and fierce as she tried not to cry. "I just thought it might be strong enough to carry one of us. And Devin, your parents are waiting for you."

Rooney chewed on her lip, hoping to keep her words inside until she could sort her tumbling thoughts, but they burst out all at once in a terrible jumble. "I thought you'd abandon us the first moment you could. It's just the type of thing you would do! So why are you being so *nice*?"

As soon as this last question slipped out, she clamped shut her mouth. It was a ridiculous accusation. To yell at someone for being kind.

"I'm always nice." Trick grinned, the corner of his lip curling impishly.

Rooney rolled her eyes. Even if she'd been wrong about him this time, she'd never apologize to Trick. It didn't change who he was deep down. Rotten at his core.

"It's decided, then." Devin came between them, smoothing things over. "We all stay, until we all can go."

"The magician may never return," Trick warned. But when Devin did not object or change her mind, he dropped his hand.

The wisp of moonlight spiraled away, and shadows swarmed as the seam above closed. Sealing them in.

Although it had been her idea to stay in the first place, folded up in the darkness, Rooney wondered if she had cursed them to remain here forever.

Only, forever might not be very long at all. She brushed her fingertips against the spot of gray on her cheekbone. Death lingered all around them.

The hairs along her arms stood on end. From nowhere came a sudden cold. The air snapped with distant crackles of blue light.

"What's that?" Devin squeaked.

The flickering came from the direction where Sorka had run off. "More trouble, no doubt," Rooney said, squinting.

"Well." Trick's black eyes reflected the strange splinters of light. "I would rather creep up on trouble than have it creep up on me."

Rooney quite agreed, and the three of them slunk forward.

The blue shimmer led the way through the woods. It zagged like lightning, so quiet without a trailing clap of thunder.

Around them, the woods shifted; the woods *changed*.

The tarnished-silver flowers bloomed before her eyes, the tips of the petals blackening before falling from the trees. As they landed upon her cheeks, they chilled her skin.

"Snow," Devin gasped.

But as the flakes fell thicker, they stung—more ice than snow. Each of the six points stabbed like needles.

Rooney, Trick, and Devin threw their hoods over their

heads, shivering beneath the icefall. It piled in drifts around them, crystals of silver and black glinting against the pitch, and above, icicles hung long and dark from the branches. A frosted-over pond curved as round as the moon between the black trees, much like the one in Warybone.

Trick brought his hand to his temple. He swallowed hard. A frosty breath plumed from his mouth as he said, "Why couldn't we have found a warm spring meadow instead?"

Though he might have been joking, Rooney suddenly wondered the same thing, and as Devin nodded, she whispered, "Maybe it's out there."

If the season in Sorka's clearing hinted at autumn with all the leafless trees, here they'd walked into a brittle-black winter.

And they'd walked right into Sorka. She stood with her back to them, black hair gusting, arms raised high.

Blue sparks crackled from her hands (no, from the *lunar mirrors* in her hands), shooting up toward the not-sky, as if she meant to slice it open. But the seam remained unbroken.

A screech of frustration rose from her throat, crashing into the night.

The darkness echoed her cry. The not-sky wrinkled, it *lowered*, coming straight toward them. The tops of the trees bowed and cracked, spilling more of the flowers-that-were-ice all around them.

Rooney, Trick, and Devin mashed together behind a thick

trunk, shuddering as the trees too squeezed tighter, the very ground beneath them eroding.

Sorka cast the unruly blue light out again. It shot through the air, wild spears of moonlight that the darkness deflected.

Mist whispered through the trees. A wind swept through too, blowing ice in their faces.

Or was it the black hole awakening?

Devin's hand lashed out, snatching hold of Trick. She struggled to speak, but her windpipe must have frozen up the same as Rooney's, for not a word escaped from between her blue-tinged lips.

Rooney leaned toward Devin, who blinked and blinked.

Frost glassed over Devin's eyes.

The edges of Rooney's vision hazed, ice crackling in their corners. But she caught sight of what had captured Devin's attention. The Monty, who'd run off into the woods when she'd woken, must have followed them here. It lay on the icy ground in their shadows, limbs stiff and still, eyes white with frost, whiskers like icicles.

Rooney scooped the little creature into her arms. She couldn't tell if it breathed.

A teardrop sprang from Rooney's eye. It froze before it could slip all the way down her cheek.

It hurt to move, but they had to!

On legs aching with cold, they fled Sorka's undisciplined magic, the treacherous winter, the coming darkness.

Though they could barely see the way, they raced for the

clearing, following the sad little whimpers of the children murmuring in unsound sleep. But suddenly Devin tugged them toward an unfamiliar part of the forest.

With great effort to push the words past the ice lining her throat, she rasped, "Summer." A shiver coursed through her. "That's where I first fell into the darkness."

They ran faster—hopeful its promise of warmth would thaw the Monty and melt the chill in their bones.

Degree by degree, the air softened, the trees thinned, and at the very edge of summer, Rooney collapsed. She held the Monty against her chest. Devin and Trick tumbled down beside her on the stretch of black sand, their bodies quaking from cold.

Waves crashed in the darkness. Or maybe that was only Rooney crashing toward sleep.

Her eyes closed. Someone found her hand and clasped it tight. She knew those hard knuckles, but she didn't let go.

The truth of it was, Trick had offered his hand just when she needed it most.

22

PETAL AND THORN

Rooney's eyes opened to darkness. She touched her cheek, unsure if she, Trick, and Devin had been frostbitten or blinded, or lost their voices for good.

Sitting up, she took a deep breath. No, obviously she could see well enough—there were Devin and Trick already awake beside her. She wiggled her fingers before her and her toes in her boots, all of which bent without pain. "Monty," she whispered, and her voice sounded as it should.

The rat lay in her lap. Its chest rose and fell. Its smudgy nose twitched.

Warm and alive. Thanks to Devin.

"What is this place?" Rooney ran her fingers through the sand.

"I don't really know," Devin admitted. "The children found me so quickly, I saw nothing more than the sand and the sea."

Setting the Monty aside, Rooney scrambled to her feet, turning. The sea spread out before her, black water, rolling waves, silver foam breaking on the shore. Another piece of Warybone mirrored in this world, just as Trick had thought.

"I don't know why they wouldn't stay here where it's warm." He stood, brushing sand from the creases of his coat.

"The sullen queen probably couldn't bear to be away from her throne," Rooney said.

Devin tilted her face up to them. "Let's explore."

And so they set off at a run.

"Watch out for sand traps!" Rooney cried, thinking they were just the sort of thing to lurk here, but even her own warning didn't slow her.

They tore down the black beach, running into the surf, then back out, their boots instantly as dry as bones. In the warmth, in the quiet, it felt like the safest place they had been since arriving. Best of all, it was free of Sorka and her erratic magic.

Trick flicked a look over his shoulder. "Race you!"

He took off without waiting to see if they would follow. Because of course they would. Rooney and Devin chased him up a small dune, the Monty trailing behind, and at the top they all stood panting.

And staring.

Another tower—no, a *lighthouse*—stood in the distance, tall and narrow and only a little crooked. It haunted the sea, lightless and dark. Waves rushed up to the great black rock it sat upon. Silver sprayed the air.

If they stood at the very top of the lighthouse, who knew how far into the darkness they might see? All its secret corners would be exposed, and in one, they might find a doorway.

Without a word, they took off down the hill, sprinting across the sand. When they reached the edge of the rock, they stopped to catch their breath. Rooney's legs burned from all the stretching. Sweat dripped down her back.

"I think I'm melting," Devin said. Loose wisps of hair curled around her face.

"Me too," Trick said, shrugging out of his coat.

They dropped their jackets to the ground, then crossed to the door of the lighthouse. Devin raised her hand. She knocked three times on the wood.

"It's abandoned. I think you can just go in," Rooney teased.

They all looked up at the lighthouse.

It leaned—only slightly, not *terribly*—toward the sea. The dark stones making up its curved walls *mostly* aligned. Black vines, blooming with tarnished-silver flowers, crawled over the stones, and though the thorns looked rather menacing, they'd only cut skin if you touched them, of course.

Which they did when Devin ripped a rather spongy grimace fruit from its stem. A drop of blood beaded on her fingertip.

"*You* can go in," Devin said, sucking on the tiny injury.

And so Rooney did, the Monty on her shoulder.

The door creaked open. A few inches of water rippled over the sunken floor, and Rooney splashed through it toward a spiraling staircase. The steps rose into darkness.

Rooney placed her hand on the railing and climbed.

"If you stumble, I'll catch you," Trick said, clunking up the stairs behind her.

And perhaps Devin realized she'd rather brave the dark lighthouse than stand at its base alone, for she came last in line. "And if *you* stumble, I'll catch *you*."

Rooney grinned.

Up and up the stairs they went, until they reached the top of the lighthouse. A window circled the whole of the room, although most of the glass was missing or cracked. Those trailing vines stabbed through the gaps, and the tarnished-silver flowers glinted, all petal and thorn.

Rooney ran forward. Trick and Devin did the same, each of them looking out in a different direction.

Below them, the darkness spread.

And it was all Rooney could see.

She spun around, fanning her flushed face with her hand. "Anything?"

"Nothing," Trick said.

The Monty leaped from Rooney's shoulder to the lantern in the room's center. It clicked its claws against metal and glass.

Rooney crossed to its side. "How do we light this thing?"

"With moonlight, I'm sure." Trick rattled all the different parts of the device. "If we had any."

"I might have just a pinch left." Devin pulled a bottle from the pocket of her skirt and shook it.

Trick beamed. With a push of his finger and a pop, a little door swung open on the lantern.

Devin tipped the bottle, and moonlight spilled into the contraption. It spread across the lens, and suddenly the darkness in the tower shattered with blue light.

Rooney, Devin, and Trick jumped back, watching the light strobe in a circle. It swung round and round, dim but glittery.

"To the windows!" Rooney cried, and they flew back to their places.

The light stretched horizontal through the darkness, poking at all those corners Rooney had hoped to see. There, the sea. There, the river. There, the clearing, the tower, the coldest winter.

And everywhere around them, the edges of the darkness loomed.

Walls rose up in all directions. Boxing them in. Closing them off from escape.

The sea did not go on and on. It flowed out from a wall of darkness. The woods did not extend indefinitely but cut off abruptly in a sheen of black. A doorway did not sit in the folds waiting for them to open it.

"No," Rooney whispered.

"No!" Devin echoed, but in a much shriller tone.

Rooney whipped her head to the side as vines lengthened

into the room. They moved slowly, harmlessly, but on their stems, the many petals of the many silver flowers began to twitch.

And, breaking from the vines, the flowers took flight.

They swarmed toward the light like six-winged moths thick with thorns-that-would-be-claws. And when Devin screamed, they converged on her, funneling straight for her mouth. She only shrieked louder.

"The light," Rooney cried, snatching up the Monty. "Turn it off! Turn it off!"

Those flowers-like-moths flocked toward Rooney. She swatted her hands through the air, but there were too many of them to stop. They set straggly-stemmed feet on her face, on her lips. They crawled through the crack of her mouth.

She spat and spat.

Trick pried at the lantern's little door. But the moonlight had trickled to the bottom of the well, and there was no retrieving it. "Let's go!"

And of course, no sooner had he spoken than the flowers-like-moths struck their thorn-and-petal wings against the air, arrowing straight for him.

He thundered down the stairs with Rooney and Devin, and they burst out into the night. Even more of those creatures filled the air, spiraling through the light as they spun round and round, angling for open mouths.

Rooney, Trick, and Devin threw their coats over their shoulders, their hoods on their heads, and they ran.

23

THE SULLEN QUEEN

Rooney pressed her lips together. She would not say another word. She'd never open her mouth again!

Not with these moths wanting to burrow their way down her throat. The moonlit lantern might have woken them, but it seemed they wanted only to find the darkest place they could—the pit of her belly.

She streaked over the black sand. Petaled wings scraped her hair, her eyelashes. They stuck most horribly to her cheeks.

Ahead, the woods appeared. Dark, dark, dark, then a pulse of blue light illuminated them, as the lighthouse lantern swung round and shone in their direction.

Her boots traveled from sand to silk as she, Trick, and Devin bore through the trees. The crisp air washed over them, and when it did, the moths swerved strangely in their flight.

They flittered and fluttered. They fell.

The chill was too much for them.

Rooney and Devin stopped, sucking air into their tired lungs. Trick coughed and spat out little moth bodies. He swiped his mouth with the back of his hand.

At their feet, silver petals lay scattered.

"No wonder they avoid this place," Trick said. "The sullen queen's magic has contaminated summer."

A lone flower-moth flopped near Rooney's toes, inching closer. "What if it spreads?"

∾

Thoughtful and anxious, they returned to the clearing, where the moonlit torches flamed blue, and the children played a game of tag. They squealed, chasing one another in and out of the trees. As if they could outrun the darkness before it kissed another gray spot on their skin.

But there was no outrunning something that held you by the tail, just as they all were, pinched within the walls of darkness.

On the throne, Sorka slouched and gloomed. Her crown lay by her bare feet, the black ribbon in her hair the only adornment.

She tilted her chin. "Tasty, aren't they? Maybe one of these days you'll listen to me."

"Not today." And with that, Rooney tugged Devin and Trick away. They dropped to the ground, spent from their ill-fated exploration.

Trick groaned, pulling a fork missing all but one tine out from under him. He rubbed his leg where the end had stabbed him. "Everything's broken here." He tossed the fork away. "Even the magic."

"Well, the sullen queen is rather moody, and I guess so is her magic," Devin said, taking the summer-grown, overripe grimace fruit from the pocket of her dress.

Rooney recalled the passing thought she'd had the night before, one that shuddered through her now. "Moody and *undisciplined*." She spoke quickly. "Earlier, she asked us what magic we'd called, and she wanted to know if we were apprenticing." Rooney looked from Devin's saucer-wide eyes to Trick's shadow-masked face. "Is that what she is?"

Devin dropped the grimace fruit. "The magician's apprentice!" she exclaimed, and then muffled her mouth with her hands.

Three pairs of eyes turned toward the throne.

Sorka scooped a lunar mirror out from the depths of her tipped-over boot (one of her many hidey-holes) and clicked open the silver lid. Most of the moonlight must have been used up by her magical fury the night before, but a dimming light still glowed from within.

It cast milk-blue shadows across Sorka's drawn face, reminding Rooney of the moonlight tumbling from the sky the previous night.

Contrary to the words in the children's creepy song,

moonlight was apparently *not* gone for good. The magician had ridden it to and from the darkness. And so must they!

But first they would have to catch it.

If only they were as sneaky as the Monty. The rat scampered across Rooney's folded ankles, its nose twitching and sniffing. It snatched up Devin's fallen grimace fruit and dashed off.

But she seemed not to care, as a dreamy look crossed her face. "I'd like to be a magician's apprentice."

"I'd rather you were than her. She's probably practicing her magic on us. She probably already cast a spell on the children, as I still don't understand why they like her."

The Monty didn't get far before one of the children pounced on it. The ragamuffin boy snickered as he stole the bruised fruit.

"If I was her, I wouldn't waste my time on that," Trick said. "I'd magic myself home."

Devin considered. "Perhaps that's what she was trying last night. And perhaps she is as bad at magic as I am at playing the violin."

Laughter burst from Rooney's throat, and it felt so strange and out of place, but she could not stop. "That poor violin. You tortured it."

Devin giggled, but then she grew serious. "I told you, I never wanted it. My parents gave it to me because they thought it was something I should learn. A path for me to follow. And I only hoped to please them. To make them proud."

"And you want to be a magician's apprentice instead?" Trick asked.

"Why not?" Devin caught the end of her braid and wrapped it around her finger. "One with a lunar mirror of my own." Devin glanced shyly at Rooney. "That's why I didn't tell when I saw you snooping outside my window."

"I wasn't snooping." *Not on purpose anyway*, Rooney thought. "I was very unsuccessfully trying to stay dry in the storm."

"Never mind that. I only wanted to befriend you. Not get you in trouble."

"And now we're all in trouble." But in that moment, Rooney felt less despair than she would have otherwise, for beside her sat a girl who might one day (who might already) be a friend.

Trick curled his fingers, never once looking up from them as he said to Devin, "I'd teach you how to catch moonlight if there was a way to do so from here. In fact, I'd swap with you if I could. Music for the mirror."

"You would not," Rooney said. She squinted at Trick as if some other boy had taken his place. "You'd never give up your mirror."

Trick cut his blackberry eyes on Rooney. "You don't know a thing about me."

"I know *many* things about you! How rotten you are."

She frowned, remembering his eagerness to see Devin return home. "How you always chase me from the best spots to gather moonlight." She winced, remembering the curl of his hand in her own. "How you always threaten me with your fists—"

"I wasn't ever going to slug you." Trick crossed his arms, dismissive of all she said. "I only wanted to keep my hands out of the way."

All those times he shook them and fisted them and raised them. Had he never meant to strike her? "You think you'll hurt them."

"I can't make music with broken-knuckled fingers, can I?"

The three of them sat in silence for a moment. Rooney didn't know what to think. All the things she thought of Trick misaligned with the boy sitting before her.

"What about you, Rooney?" Trick asked at last. "What do you long for?" With his arms still folded and his brows scrunched up, his scrutiny felt like a test.

"My mirror." That wasn't the whole of it, though. She wanted so much more than that, for her mirror could not hold a conversation or her hand. It could not laugh or argue or cry. It could not listen. But Rooney spoke none of these things aloud.

To want a thing also meant to fear not having it.

"My mirror," she said again, most decidedly, before Trick could reply. They had more important things to discuss than what they wanted. None of it mattered unless they escaped.

"If only we knew what Sorka wanted most, we could trade it for the mirrors. Then we'd be able to gather moonlight, enough to carry us all out of the darkness as it did the magician." Rooney turned to look at Sorka once again.

The sullen queen now sat on the ground, her back against the onyx throne. The lunar mirror was out of sight. A book rested open on her lap. But she wasn't reading it. Quite terribly, she was tearing out its pages. One, two, three, she ripped them from the spine and then tossed the book to the side.

"She never gives back anything she takes. At least not until she's grown bored with it," Devin said.

"Or broken it." Rooney cringed as Sorka folded one of the torn-out pages and cut into it with scissors. Rooney imagined Sorka smashing their mirrors just as destructively. "We can't wait any longer."

"We'll have to take them back," Trick said.

Rooney swung to face him. "Well, you do know a thing or two about stealing."

Trick shot her a crooked smile. "Thank you."

"It wasn't a compliment," Rooney huffed, while Devin started giggling again. It was all Rooney could do to keep a straight face and not join her.

And she might have. Oh, she might have.

Except a sudden crack rang out in the darkness, and everyone fell silent at once.

THIS EVER-DARK NIGHT

Rooney waited for the sound to come again, but there was only the quiet left in its wake.

And the air thickening.

And the ground trembling.

Rooney, Trick, and Devin jumped to their feet. The Monty scrambled up Rooney's leg, and the children, who'd been playing moments before, now dashed from the tree line into the clearing. Rooney's eyes went immediately to the throne, but there was no sign that Sorka had caused the disruption.

The girl seemed to be in a world of her own. She'd finished cutting shapes into the pages torn from the book and unfolded them one by one, stringing them on thin threads. When she was done, she climbed onto the arm of her onyx throne, pushed up to her tiptoes, and pinned the threads to the drooping tent of darkness. With their sharp, pointed corners, the little papers dangled like over-large snowflakes.

Or were they stars? Ones that Sorka hoped to see again too?

Maybe Sorka's unhurried manner should have reassured Rooney, but it made her all the more nervous.

"Is the magician back so soon?" Devin asked warily. "We aren't ready yet."

The air had the same feel as when the magician had come—that heaviness when Rooney breathed in. But the cold wasn't pressing close. The moonlight wasn't streaming gently down. "I don't think so."

"But the darkness has let someone in." Sorka skipped up behind them, uttering these words in her low, creepy voice.

Dread gripped Rooney.

Another child must have been snatched from the streets of Warybone.

With the Monty in hand, Rooney hurried after Sorka. She'd get some answers from her now. She just had to.

But a group of children gathered round so that Rooney could not elbow her way close to their sullen queen. They waved moonlit torches. They struck up their fiddles and bows and placed their flutes to their lips. Discordant music streamed forth, and their lilting voices rose into the night, tinged with both excitement and sorrow.

Come out, my friends
Come out, my foes
If you're here
No one else knows

Rooney wanted to cover her ears, but it wouldn't have helped. The words tumbled through her head anyway.

Try if you want
To gather moonlight
But it's gone for good
In this ever-dark night

"Sorka," Rooney called, daring to use her name once again. "Please wait." But this time, Sorka led the line of children toward the woods, singing loudest of them all. A welcoming. A warning.

It's death you've found
And we must confess
There's no escaping
The plentiful darkness

A few of the children circled back, tugging at Rooney's sleeves, linking elbows with Devin, nudging Trick—urging them to sing along with them. "Come!" they said.

Rooney squirmed out of their grasp and pulled Devin and Trick away with her. "Now's our chance." She glanced at the empty throne, with those paper ornaments suspended above it. "Look for the mirrors. *Find* the mirrors."

She passed the Monty to Devin and took a step toward the woods, where she could see the last of the children slipping between the trees, black silhouettes against the misty blue light.

"You're going after them?" Devin clutched the little rat to her chest. "But why?"

"We need to learn all we can."

Though Rooney wanted nothing more than to search for her mirror, she'd have to trust Devin and Trick. For she needed to see if the way *into* the darkness might also be the way *out*.

Rooney raced toward the woods, following the high notes of music and the soft glow of the torches.

Despite Sorka's claims that there was no escaping, Rooney would not give up on returning to Warybone with her mirror in hand.

When she reached the children, she became the very last in their unruly line, but she did not join in on their song and dance. Some poor child was falling, and falling, and falling to the same fate as her own. Her heart felt heavy at the thought.

As she hurried after the group, the faintest glimmer of stars shone above. They reflected in the river rushing silently by.

Rooney watched Sorka. The girl marched on and on, her arms flung wide, her ribboned hair flying wild around her shoulders. For all the time she spent alone, sulking on her throne, seeing her so lively, so animated, seemed most strange.

Sorka never once glanced back as she led the peculiar parade through the woods. Instead, she stared and stared at the crack of sky so far out of reach.

A body tumbled through the pitch, a straight shot down from above. Rooney could just see the outline of the girl's belled skirt, her arms flailing helplessly, and her legs kicking at air.

All the singing stopped abruptly, interrupted by the howling of the girl dropping through the plentiful darkness. She shrieked and shouted, headed right for the points of the trees.

"Someone has to help her!" Rooney cried, but nothing could be done.

The girl was falling too fast. The trees were crowded too close together.

In fact, they drew closer still, tilting toward one another and overlapping their branches in a perfect pattern. Their limbs knit together like dozens of interlocked fingers, angled from the sky all the way to the ground. In this manner, they formed the longest, the steepest, the strangest of slides.

And just in time.

The girl plunged through the air, flopping into the cradle of trees. Her howl cut off, the wind knocked from her lungs. She slipped and slid her way down the slide, moving so quickly her face was no more than a blur, her short dark hair whipping around her head.

Faster and faster, she descended in an almost vertical drop before the slide curved and twisted. She bumped her way along, swooping down, down, down, and spilled onto the ground.

The mess of her hair tangled across her face, but it was not long enough to cover her scowling mouth and the thin puckered scar at the corner of her lip. Rooney narrowed her eyes at the girl.

It was none other than Bridget Mullen.

25

UNSTABLE MAGIC

The night crouched closer around Rooney, a smaller space than it had been before. Their surroundings pinched and squeezed, closing in, and the brief show of stars winked out—all the children sealed into the darkness once again. With Bridget.

How horrible!

Rooney would have preferred any other face to the one glowering before her, and she pushed her way backward through the children until she stood at the edge of the group, beyond the dim flare of the torches. Beyond Bridget's roving eye. Rooney was not ready to confront this roughhouse boy just yet. Not in front of everyone.

From her bent-legged position on the ground, Bridget glared up at the children, who had gathered round and watched her with curiosity. Rubbing a small cut on her cheek, she shot to her feet, wobbling a little as she did so, out of sorts from her long tumble through the air. With a steadying breath, she spun a circle. Her eyes tracked through the darkness, taking in the woods, the children . . . the quiet.

Then she broke it quite suddenly, quite thoroughly, shouting, "What in all the wretched world is this witch-darkened place?"

Sorka stalked forward, the group of children parting to let her through. She gazed down her pointy nose as she said, "Friend or foe?"

Bridget stamped her foot. She screamed. Answer enough, it seemed to Rooney. Bridget was not going to play along.

Sorka turned away with a quick flick of her wrist. The trees that had formed the silken slide parted, fanning up and away from one another once again. It was wonderful, Rooney thought, the way they spread apart like the wings of a great black bird. She would have liked to ride them out of the darkness—or have them catapult her out of it.

One of the branches swatted Bridget from behind as it rose, sending her stumbling forward. And that was even more wonderful—seeing Bridget's face redden in anger. She screamed again, but that didn't stop two of the children from coming up to each side of her and linking their arms with her own. She squirmed and wiggled, but they kept hold of her as if she might not be steady enough to walk alone. They skipped forward when Sorka started back through the woods.

Rooney ducked behind the trees until Bridget had passed, then trailed last in line once again. Bridget shouted and yelled as the children marched her along.

Rather unexpectedly, Bridget's fury echoed everything Rooney felt but had pushed deep inside.

She didn't want to think about it—that they had anything in common—and slipped out of the disorderly line and into the trees. Devin and Trick might still be picking through Sorka's things. She needed to drag them away before Sorka caught them at it. Rooney ran.

But when Rooney burst into the clearing, she immediately realized she hadn't needed to rush. Bridget's shouts could be heard even at a distance, booming through the trees and warning Trick and Devin of the group's impending return. Already, they stood in the shadows away from the throne, hands behind their backs, as if to hide that they'd been snooping only moments before.

As if to hide what they'd taken back! Hope stretched in Rooney's chest.

She dashed to their sides. "Well? Let me see them. Let me have mine."

Trick all but ignored her, staring at the children spilling into the clearing, mouth agape when he saw Bridget in their midst. A mixture of surprise and gladness. With a frown, Rooney turned toward Devin.

Devin spread her empty hands in front of her. "We couldn't find them."

Rooney wanted to scream as loudly as Bridget. "Not even one?"

"She must have the mirrors in her pockets or tucked away in some hidden cubby." Devin scratched at the gray patch on her neck.

"Good thing Bridget's here. She'll know what to do." Trick edged closer to the group, and Devin followed.

With her frown deepening, Rooney tagged after. "We've already got a plan."

"Not without the mirrors, we don't," Trick said.

Rooney buttoned her lips, though she would have liked to point out that their unsuccessful retrieval was Trick's fault, not her own.

"Either way, we need to do something, and quick. The darkness . . ." Devin shivered. "Its walls are closing in."

Rooney recalled the moment Bridget had dropped from the sky—the sensation of the pitch pressing nearer.

She thought Trick would deny it, just to be contradictory, but he nodded. "Maybe there's too many of us."

As if each new child shrank the space around them and sucked up more of the air. It made Rooney all the more anxious to escape this undisciplined, this *unstable*, magic.

And the sullen queen who wielded it.

Still ahead of the other children, Sorka proceeded directly to the onyx throne and hopped up into it. If Devin and Trick had disturbed any of her possessions, she didn't seem to notice.

And still, with all those many trinkets, Sorka always demanded more. She leaned greedily toward the newest arrival, her long hair tumbling over her shoulders, and said, "What have you brought me?"

With a shove and a kick, Bridget tore loose from the children beside her. They scampered away. "Absolutely nothing!"

"How rude. How foe-like." Sorka plucked her crown up from the ground and set it on her head, as if that might make her authority clear.

Seemingly unimpressed, Bridget crossed her arms. "And you, how horrid! Are those spiderwebs strung across your face?"

Rooney rubbed her cheek. She didn't think there was anything funny about the gray clinging to each and every one of them, but Trick snorted. Rooney elbowed him. With Bridget and him together, the plentiful darkness would not only be awful, soon it would be insufferable.

Sorka sneered at Bridget. "You little rat."

Of all the things to call Bridget, Sorka couldn't have chosen a better insult. Bridget flinched, and this time Rooney snorted and Trick elbowed her.

A sharp glint sparked in Sorka's eye, and the earth began to ripple.

"What's happening?" Bridget froze in place, looking at the ground so she did not see Sorka jump down from the platform.

"I'm taking what's mine." Sorka reached into Bridget's pocket and snatched up whatever lay within.

Bridget threw a fist, but not in time. Sorka was already settling back on her throne and inspecting the silver object in her hand.

"Her lunar mirror," Rooney whispered, reminded of just how Bridget had commanded the roughhouse boys to take Rooney's own.

Only, Rooney felt no satisfaction. Not if it meant Sorka had claimed another one.

Besides, Bridget hardly seemed to care about the mirror anyway. She asked for (shouted for) Trick in her next breath. "Where's Trick? What's become of him?"

Trick stepped forward, at the ready to show himself and defend his friend from the still-rumbling ground, but Devin clung to his sleeve. "You'll only make it worse. Just wait."

With a sweep of her arm, Sorka commanded the silken ground, knocking Bridget off her feet. Bridget rolled away from the throne before she managed to dig in her heels and regain her footing.

A tendril of silk writhed up from the ground like a new tree sprouting. Bridget scrambled forward but not far. The silk looped around her ankle, twisting and tightening and holding her in place.

She yelled again for Trick.

Perhaps it was because Bridget seemed to care so little for the theft of her mirror that it lost its appeal for Sorka. With widening eyes, Rooney watched as Sorka tossed it onto a stack of trinkets, where it rested among a music box, a toy soldier, a teakettle, and other assorted objects. Then she called to the children, asking that they entertain her with a game of hide-and-seek. One by one, they ran into the woods.

With Sorka properly occupied, Trick waited no more, hurrying over to Bridget's side. Rooney (quite grumpily) and Devin (quite curiously) gathered next to him.

"Bridget." Trick bent down, tugging at the length of silk, though it refused to budge. "I never thought the magician could catch you."

"You *are* here. I knew it. I told those boys I'd find you, never mind the bruises and blood. And who says that witch caught me? I *let* her take me." Her green eyes flicked over to Rooney. "Oh, you. Ratty de Barra."

"Her name's Rooney," Devin said, as if Bridget might have misspoken (she hadn't). "And I'm Devin Hayes. Hello."

"Hello?" Bridget grouched. "I've just been rolled all about and witch-magicked to the ground, and you say hello like everything's pleasant as can be? What sort of nonsense is that?"

"Don't speak to her that way," Rooney said. "In fact, don't bother to speak at all." Bridget's mouth snapped shut, and Rooney was feeling good and pleased with herself when she heard a little squeak. Even better. "Unless you want to say hello to Monty."

All eyes fell on the rat sitting by Rooney's ankle. Bridget

drew as far back as she could, clutching her rat-nibbled finger to her chest. She hissed.

"Oh, Bridge, relax," Trick said, giving up on the slippery knots he hadn't managed to untangle. He cocked his head at Rooney. "Can you get the rat to help out?"

"Don't want to," Rooney grumbled, but if she did nothing, Bridget would only begin shouting again. She looked at the Monty and sighed. "Go ahead. Chew her loose if you can."

It skittered over to Bridget, who shuddered in fright (much to Rooney's delight), and in the same manner it had gnawed on the tree branch to release Trick, it chomped the silken binding until Bridget could squirm free.

Without a thank-you to the rat, she popped up to her feet, grinning at Trick. "Now that I've found you, let's hack our way out of this witch-scarf realm." From her boot, she grabbed a little knife, and with a triumphant smile (and a defiant laugh as Rooney and Devin shouted *no, no, no*), she threw it, end over end, toward the ground.

26

SIDE BY SIDE

Snatching the rat, Rooney shrank back, waiting for the knife to stab the earth. For the fog to hiss up from the wounded silk. For the darkness to rush forth and envelop them again, just as the black hole almost had.

But Trick lunged forward, right in the knife's path. It angled toward his thigh. Devin shrieked.

Just in time, he swept his coat out like the wing of a bat, swatting the knife. It struck the burr-roughened fabric and then fell harmlessly and soundlessly to the ground.

Rooney eyed the blade. "It might have hit you—"

"What did you go and do that for?" Bridget grumbled. (For once Rooney was grateful for the interruption so Trick would not have the silly notion that she cared about him.)

"We already tried to slice through the darkness." Trick scrubbed the spot of gray above his eyebrow. "With lousy results."

"It marked us for death," Devin whispered, pointing out the patches on their faces and neck.

"Hmpf." Bridget retrieved her knife, slashing it angrily through the air before shoving it back in her boot. "We're not dead yet."

Trick might have been willing to put his trust in Bridget, but Rooney wasn't impressed. "Oh, she'll know what to do, will she?" Rooney muttered to the Monty.

Despite her hushed tone, Trick must have heard her mocking his words. "She's gotten me out of a scrape a time or two. She's got my back." He said it as if he knew that Rooney had not; did not.

"I'll do the same this time too," Bridget said smugly. "And all the times to come."

For once, it wasn't Bridget's self-assured words or her slick little smile that bothered Rooney. It was the realization that underneath all Bridget's tough exterior, there were steadfast layers of loyalty and love. She had sought out the darkness. She must truly have cared about Trick.

In a way that no one cared about Rooney.

The anger and loneliness and fear that had been building inside her exploded at Trick. "You're the one who got us *into* this scrape!"

"You got *yourself* into it," he said. "Stop blaming everyone else."

Rooney angled away from Trick. She didn't want to bother with him just then or hear anything he hoped to say to her. Bridget stood before her now, and Rooney couldn't hold back any longer. "All you do is cause trouble. If you hadn't told the boys to steal my mirror, we might never have crossed paths with the magician. We wouldn't be here. We wouldn't be miserable."

Although, that last point wasn't exactly true. Rooney had been rather miserable before, but she wasn't about to admit it.

Devin, who had been opening and closing, opening and closing her mouth as they bickered, finally broke in. "Stop arguing. Stop fighting." She stumbled over her words when everyone stood there awkwardly and crossly, looking anywhere but at one another. "And maybe I shouldn't think so or say so, but I'm glad you're all here. That you're my friends. If you hadn't come, I'd be stuck here . . . with them."

They all turned toward the woods where Sorka and the other children crouched and sneaked and hid. Resigned to their dire situation, even as the darkness closed around them.

Rooney's heart clenched—Devin thought her a friend—but it broke a little too. "Be *cautious* of who you trust." Rooney glared at Trick, then looked back to Devin. "They aren't our friends, not really."

She meant to stop there. That was all Devin needed to know. But the secrets she'd only shared with the Monty came tumbling out now that there was someone else listening. "They turned me away from joining the roughhouse boys. Bridget chose Trick when he caught the most moonlight."

Just thinking of that warm, clear night brought an ache to Rooney's chest. How she'd done her very best, chasing the moonlight and filling her lunar mirror. How it hadn't been good enough. Trick with just that tiny smidgen more, never mind the slivered crack in his mirror, and Bridget clapping him on the back. Rooney had run off. She hadn't looked back.

She shook the memory from her head. "Now they're always set on besting me, not befriending me."

Her words hung in the air. She could not take them back, and the thought that Trick and Bridget would use this admission against her too—to tease her and taunt her—twisted her stomach into knots.

"It was all for fun," Trick said. "You're the one who shut us out. Like the moonlight belonged only to you, and you couldn't stand that I matched you."

"Always acting like you're too good for us," Bridget said.

"Like you have to do everything yourself."

"And always so gloomy."

Their back-and-forth words struck Rooney harder and harder. "What?" she sputtered, unable to wholly deny their accusations even though she wanted nothing more. She *was* rather gloomy. Maybe she sometimes *did* think she knew best. Being all alone, there had never been anyone to object.

"I'm sorry we're in this mess, but that's why I took your mirror." Trick's jaw sharpened as he admitted, "I knew you'd come looking for it. And for some rotten reason, I wanted you to."

Rooney had no words, only a swirl of confusion in her head. The Monty slipped up to her shoulder, bumping its nose to her cheek.

Trick locked his blackberry eyes onto Rooney's. Oh, they were still sour as could be, but they were also wide and clear and completely unmasked. "I wanted you to be one of us." As if he'd gotten too soft, he added rather gruffly, "If you weren't so stubborn, you would have been ages ago."

Bridget didn't agree with him, but she didn't disagree with him either. She scratched her ear.

Rooney blinked, looking at the toes of her boots. *Could it be true?*

They'd been down here all these days, side by side. And yes, they'd fought, but not horribly. And not always. They'd faced off against Sorka. They'd plotted ways to escape. They hadn't really behaved as foes might be expected to.

Devin slipped her hand into Rooney's. Trick did not, but she remembered the feel of his fingers tucked around her own, and she felt no less warmed by his words (no matter how prickly they'd been spoken). She raised her chin. She found an unexpected grin on her face. "You should have just said so. You should have told me."

"Well, I said it now." Trick's lip hitched. "Because I'm always nice."

Bridget rolled her eyes beneath her long bangs. Devin squeezed Rooney's hand.

For the first time, standing together with this group under the black not-sky and within the dark woods, Rooney no longer felt *untogether*. Trick and Devin (and the Monty, of course) were next to her—they were *with* her when she needed them most. And she realized she was *with* them, for friendship must go both ways for it to be true.

And though she still wasn't so sure about Bridget, maybe that could come in time.

If, if, if they found their way back home to Warybone.

27

THE SNEAKIEST

The moonlit glow flickered in Rooney's chest once more—warmer, steadier, fuller than it had been in so long. It shifted inside her, from the embers of hope to something much less familiar—the sturdiness of trust. The magician could have swept down right then, and Rooney wouldn't have felt the cold. She wouldn't have trembled either, for she would have her newly found *friends* standing shoulder to shoulder beside her.

All the more reason she had to be ready for the magician's return. She wanted so fiercely to protect them.

"Trick," Rooney said, wondering at how different his name sounded on her tongue when she was not thinking of slugging him. And then she made an even bigger gesture (though it was a very small thing indeed) to test the sound of Bridget's name in an attempt to smooth some of the bad feelings between them. "Tell Bridget all that's happened."

They gathered close as he began, with Devin or Rooney filling in bits and pieces here or there that he might have otherwise glossed over—about the encroaching darkness, about Sorka and the magician, about their plotting.

After the story had been laid before her, Bridget tucked her hair crisply behind her ears. "It's the mirrors we need. They'll be our way out of here."

Rooney had thought that Bridget might attempt to take charge of things, the way she bossed Colin and Sim. But in agreeing with Rooney's plan, Bridget seemed to be trying to get along.

"We can't find their mirrors," Devin reminded her.

"But we can find *mine*," Bridget said.

Rooney had almost forgotten about Bridget's mirror, tossed so casually away by Sorka. It rested somewhere in that pile beside the throne, which the sullen queen had returned to.

She cut her eyes at them.

Devin grabbed the sleeve of Trick's coat. "Oh, she knows we're up to something."

Together, they spun around and away from Sorka, which was no less suspicious, but when Rooney stole a quick look over her shoulder some minutes later, she saw that Sorka had turned her cheek, disinterested. Two of the children—a shadow-haired girl who could most often be found gazing into the silken river when she'd been tasked with collecting water, and a scrawny boy who spent most of his time high in the trees picking flowers for Sorka's silver crown—had climbed up on the throne's little platform and set about braiding the sullen queen's hair. She closed her eyes, much like a spoiled cat anticipating a good scratching behind its ears.

"We better not wait. She'll guess what we're after and hide that mirror too," Devin said.

"Yes." Rooney knew Sorka might have shut her eyes, but that didn't mean she wasn't keenly aware of them. "And we'll have to send the sneakiest one of us."

"That's me," Trick said at the same time Bridget placed her hands on her hips and proclaimed, "I'm the sneakiest."

Rooney smiled. She had someone else in mind entirely. "You won't like this, I'm afraid," she said to Bridget.

"Of course you think it should be you." Bridget pressed her lips together, as if she'd been wrong to give Rooney a chance at setting things right between them.

"No, not me." Rooney tilted her head, indicating the Monty perched on her shoulder.

Instead of recoiling as Rooney thought she might, Bridget leaned forward, her eyes sharp as she grinned. "Oh, if nothing else, little beasts make for good sneaks."

The Monty preened, running its paws across its smudgy nose. Perhaps the rat thought itself fierce for being called a beast.

"Snatch the lunar mirror from the pile beside the throne," Rooney told the Monty, setting it on the ground. "But don't let the sullen queen catch whisker or tail of you."

The rat scampered off, and it was all Rooney could do not to watch it advance toward the throne, but that would surely draw Sorka's attention.

"Come on." Perhaps Trick had the same thought, for he said, "Let's keep ourselves busy."

He led them toward the edge of the woods where (after reassuring Bridget it would not kill her, no really, it wasn't rotted and gross) they began gathering grimace fruit from the lowest of the trees' branches.

"I'd give anything for a potato pot pie," Devin said mournfully. "My father's pies are the very best."

Rooney's mouth began to water. "Ack, don't torture me. Don't make me wish for something I can't have."

"You *can* have it," Devin said. "Because we will return home, and I'll have you all over for supper."

Rooney froze with her arm outstretched toward a grimace fruit. Trick glanced at his hands, and Bridget twisted her lips to the side with an unreadable expression on her face. The air hung all the heavier in their momentary silence, each of them caught on the word *home*.

"Bone marrow stew. That's what my ma made best, cooking while my pop played the piano." As if to cover the yearning in his voice, Trick pulled a small wrinkly fruit from its branch, and, quite appropriately, he grimaced.

"Bread for me. My parents were bakers, you know." Bridget paused, and then said quickly, "Before the feather flu took them."

Rooney's heart lurched. "I'm sorry." And oh, she meant it sincerely and truly. She hadn't known this tragedy had touched Bridget (and Trick too, most likely), but it seemed something she should have realized sooner. If she'd been thinking about anyone other than herself.

"I miss the blackberries," she whispered. But what she meant was, *I'm sorry, I'm sorry. I miss my parents too.*

"And all we've got is this witch-worked fruit." Scrunching up her face, Bridget took her first bite of the grimace fruit. She chewed. She swallowed. "Though it isn't half-bad."

"Told you," Trick said.

Bridget stuck out her tongue, which was stained purple with juice, but no sooner had she done so than she let out a little scream.

As sneakily as promised, the Monty had found them at the edge of the woods. It bristled around Bridget's ankles. She lifted her foot, its shadow falling atop the rat with the threat that her boot would follow.

"Don't you dare," Rooney warned. She bent in a great hurry, dumping an armful of grimace fruits on the ground. Trick, Devin, and Bridget leaned over her shoulders as she held out her hands and accepted the rat's offering.

28

THE WORLD ABOVE

Rooney's pulse leaped. Cupped in her palms, she held a round silver object. It was cool to the touch.

Except, when she looked closely through the gloom, she saw she wasn't holding a lunar mirror—only something that could be mistaken for one. The Monty had brought her an ordinary pocket watch that no longer told the time.

"Good try," she said, so as not to discourage the rat. "But you'll need to go again. The lunar mirror is what we want."

And so it dashed off—three times more, three times unsuccessful—bringing back a golden pillbox, a stringless metal yo-yo, and a silver locket on a thin, broken-clasped chain.

"Oh, Monty," Rooney sighed as she accepted this last item. "You might be sneaky, but you are not being properly selective. The *mirror*."

As the rat slunk away once again, she looked down at the necklace in her hand. A moment later, a sudden clatter broke the quiet. Trinkets spilled from the pile beside the throne. Smudgy nose twitching, the Monty scrabbled out of the wreckage, charging away from the little avalanche it had caused.

Sorka stormed to her feet. The darkness cringed—a shuddering, a pinching—contracting the space around them.

The children near her throne scattered as her cheeks burned red and the black ribbons at the ends of her braids lashed like furious snakes. "You rotten thief!" she shouted, and her words too, booming so loud, shook the darkness, gathering it closer around them.

What would happen if it continued to shrivel and squeeze?

A tickle of claustrophobia teased Rooney, but she shoved it aside as best she could. The rat fled with an object in its paws—maybe Bridget's mirror at last! Dashing away from the woods, Rooney and the others hurried to meet it.

At the same time, Sorka jumped to the ground. It rippled under her feet. The rat scampered against the wavering silk, but its long claws were unable to take hold and carry itself away. Sorka pounced, lifting the rat up by the scruff of its skinny neck.

"Careful!" Rooney cried.

The ground stilled, but Sorka's temper only flared brighter. She let the Monty dangle there from the ends of her pinched fingers, its little feet kicking. "Oh, I don't much like rats. But I *very* much dislike thieves." She glared straight at Rooney.

Bridget trundled forward, big steps for a small girl. She wore her sternest face, eyes cutting under her stick-straight bangs. "You're the thorny thief. That mirror is mine!"

Standing steady beside Bridget, who somehow even *breathed* with authority, Rooney could not help but feel stronger.

And Sorka—unbelievably—seemed to shrink, just as the darkness had. "I'm not talking about the mirror." The Monty dropped the trinket, which Bridget dived for and quickly scooped up as Sorka continued. "I'm talking about the locket."

Rooney glanced at the thin chain threaded around her fingers. She rubbed her thumb over the dulled surface, surprised that this broken ornament had made Sorka so upset. Unless it meant something more to her, the way Rooney would always love her charm bracelet of stars, even though she no longer owned it.

She bowed her head over the locket, and dim blue light fell over an etching on its surface.

A thorny stem, just like the design on the lunar mirrors.

Heart thumping fast, Rooney clicked opened the locket. Within, instead of tiny portraits or a curled strand of hair, lay a small mirror. One that offered no reflection.

A lunar mirror.

Rooney gasped at the wonder of finding such a thing

in the locket. At the horror of finding the glass lined with cracks.

Sorka lowered her arm, releasing the Monty, who scampered away. "I thought I lost it for good."

"What's so special about it?" Rooney asked.

Keeping something back, Sorka shook her head. Silver petals fell from her crown. "Once, it contained stardust, but that's long gone."

A shiver coursed through Rooney. This hope of hers—to catch the light of a star—shimmered like a possibility instead of a dream. Something her parents had longed for, though they had only gathered its imitation by way of silver charms and a telescope's glass. "Stardust!"

"Can it really be caught?" Devin pressed close to Rooney, as awestruck as Trick when he spoke of making music. "My mother always told tales of golden lassos woven from stardust and crowns glittering with starlight, but I thought they were fables."

"My father swore my mother's wedding ring was made from the dust of a falling star," Trick said wistfully.

"Those are just stories." But a question lingered in Bridget's words.

"*True* stories," Sorka insisted, eyeing the locket.

Rooney thought Sorka might lunge for it with greedy fingers, the way she'd snatched away the lunar mirrors. But Sorka only stood there, acting nothing like herself.

Or maybe more herself than ever. Rooney had to admit

she did not always see the whole of a person. She hadn't with Trick, that was certain. And for all Sorka's outbursts, she rather had a way with the children—how she gathered them to her and read stories, how she magicked their silken bed-rolls at night, how she played with them so they might smile and forget, even for a little while, all that they missed from home.

All Sorka must miss.

Rooney thought of the way Sorka looked at the sky as Bridget fell through it, and all the stars she'd shaped from the pages of a book. She'd flung such vibrant magic in the winter woods, her emotions tangled within it.

Sorka wanted to find her way out of the darkness too.

"Well, how do we go about snatching stardust, then?" Bridget held the lunar mirror the Monty had dropped and looked at it this way and that.

With an unsettling frown, Sorka righted her crown. "I said it's been caught, not that *you* could catch it."

"Maybe I could, if I stole your locket for myself." Bridget wiggled her fingers as if she meant to take it from Rooney.

"Don't be rotten to each other, all right?" Devin pleaded.

"Oh, but I am rotten," Sorka said, her grayed skin stretching as she smiled. "The darkness has sunken into my bones. It runs through my veins. It's part of me more surely than anything else."

But Rooney had seen something in Sorka, a glimpse of a girl who needed protecting as much as the rest of them.

Rooney thrust out her arm. Though Bridget grumbled beside her, Rooney held the locket aloft, hoping it was just what Sorka needed most. The necklace itself, but more so, the offering of it, and nothing asked for in return.

Sorka lifted her hand, hesitant. She must have thought Rooney would snatch the locket away at the last moment. But Rooney wouldn't; she didn't.

When Sorka's fingers closed around the chain, the darkness around them sighed. Branches swayed in the woods, though there wasn't any breeze, and far off, the river rushed. Cold came in waves from Sorka's pale skin as she gazed at the locket.

Then her voice broke, scratchy and unwilling—and sad. "All I want is to see the stars again. Not from the depths of darkness, but from the world above."

29

AT LAST, AT LAST

ooney stared off into the pitch. It draped around them, a too-tight embrace. She did not want to remain here in the shrinking darkness, so far away from Warybone.

And Sorka had finally admitted she felt the same.

The confession seemed genuine, but Rooney scratched the splotch of gray on her cheek, unsure, uncertain, unsatisfied. A whisper of cold swept through her.

Winter cold.

At the edge of the clearing farthest from the throne, the highest tree branches swished back and forth, and the silver flowers began to fall and blacken. Crystals of ice cut through the air.

Winter did not belong here.

The chill ghosted Rooney's breath and stole her voice. She pointed a shaky finger to the sliver of the woods where winter brushed against the border of autumn. Devin and Bridget widened their eyes in alarm.

"Winter has come a-crawling," one of the children, paused in their play, called out.

Sorka tucked the necklace into the pocket of her dress and patted it softly. Without a word, she climbed onto the arm of the onyx throne and reached for the paper ornaments she'd hung up so recently. One by one, she tore them down, plucking her handmade stars from the not-sky. She crushed them in her fist and hurled them about. Her fragile dreams lay scattered at her feet.

"What's happening?" Devin asked, wary of the silvering woods.

Rooney scooped up the closest of Sorka's fallen stars. She tried to smooth it again, but the paper was rumpled and creased beyond repair. "The darkness is closing in, isn't it? Squeezing the seasons and all of us together."

"Spring is already gone," Sorka whispered.

Rooney startled at the idea of something so wondrous ceasing to exist. But she had seen its destruction for herself. Those cobblestones all broken. That tower all crooked.

Devin had said, *Whatever was at the end of this road is gone.*

The black hole had gobbled spring up.

"It's lost in the darkness." Sorka lowered her voice even further so the children couldn't hear her. "And it's only a matter of time before we're smothered too."

Devin staggered back, bumping into Bridget, who slung

her arm roughly (almost protectively) around her shoulder. Rooney would have liked some reassurance as well. Some sign that Sorka knew how to hold the wintry darkness back. But it must have been Sorka's undisciplined magic that brought this danger all the closer.

No longer was it just a strange feeling, a far-off threat. If they didn't escape, and soon, the darkness would fold them into their graves.

"Do you remember what you asked us?" Rooney swallowed, digging deep to find her strength. "Friend or foe?"

Sorka offered another lean smile. "I remember everything."

"Then you should remember we came as *friends*."

Rooney glanced at Devin and Trick (and Bridget, who hadn't actually answered the question at all, but never mind that). The three of them waited and watched. Sorka took a long look at them too. Her jaw worked back and forth.

"If we're all supposed to be friends . . . ," Rooney began, knowing they weren't, not really. Not *yet*. But she was trying at least. "If we're supposed to tell each other the truth of things, then we must be honest with you too." Sorka narrowed her eyes, and Rooney finished. "About our plan for escape."

Behind her, Bridget grumbled. Devin, however, said loud and clear, "Yes, tell her."

Everyone slipped closer, and Rooney shared the not-wholly-full-and-finished plan—to use the lunar mirrors to catch whatever bits of light they could at the very next opportunity (whenever, however, that might come) and follow it out of this place.

"So you see why we need the mirrors," Rooney said at the end of the telling. "Not to strike out at the darkness but to bring in the light."

Sorka frowned. With gray-tipped fingers, she touched the decay along her collarbone.

"So you see why we need *you*," Devin amended with a small smile, in the same manner she had looked at Rooney from the window—so eager to keep the trouble away from others, even as she plunged right into it herself.

"To use my magic," Sorka said stiffly, perhaps thinking it was the only thing someone might want from her.

"No, not that," Trick said (though Rooney would not have dismissed it so quickly). "To lead the children. They'll follow you anywhere because they trust you." And what he didn't say but expressed all the same was that he would trust in Sorka too.

Avoiding the whisper of winter at the woods' edge, the children played close by, hands of cards with incomplete decks and made-up rules, wooden puzzles that could never be finished for all the missing pieces, and games of catch with . . . a round silver object.

Rooney's mouth dropped open. "You gave them one of our mirrors!"

"I might have." Sorka grinned. "I did."

Oh, Rooney had tried so hard to set things right, and all

for nothing. She dashed away from Sorka and the others, tearing into the middle of the clearing. A streak of silver shot through the air.

"Be careful," she cried. The mirrors were the only things that could save them.

The children laughed as she hollered, tossing the mirror over her head, changing their game from catch to keep-away. When it soared by again, Rooney leaped for it. And missed.

A blur of movement swept past, a shadow grazing her arm—Bridget, with her cropped black hair and dark dress. She tackled the child who'd just caught the mirror and wrestled it from his grip. The boy cackled, as if he was well used to such mischief (and was usually the culprit).

Bridget pushed to her feet, casting a look over her shoulder so severe the boy ran.

"Here," she said gruffly, plopping the mirror into Rooney's hand.

It fit just right in her palm. Not any old mirror. *Her* mirror. Rooney's heart swelled. Despite the chill in the air, the moonlit fire in her chest burned, so bright the others must have been able to see its glow.

She traced her thumb over the familiar groove and then the silver-etched thorn. At last, at last, her mirror was returned to her.

Rescued, most surprisingly, by Bridget Mullen.

The gesture was so unexpected. Rooney lifted her head,

but before she could offer even the smallest of thanks, Bridget stalked over to Sorka.

"We need one more," Bridget said, not a bit out of breath from her tussle with the boy.

"Two more," Devin said, linking her arm with Bridget's, making it seem so easy to align with someone. To befriend someone.

Sorka squirmed on the throne. Rooney was sure she would deny them.

But from under the silken cushion, Sorka withdrew a lunar mirror. Trick's mirror. She looked at it, undecided. Carefully, cautiously, Trick reached out and eased it from her hand.

Sorka sighed. "You all are determined to be disappointed. Don't you know how many times I've tried?"

Rooney rounded on the throne, for once knowing exactly what she wanted to say. "A thousand, I'm sure. But you haven't had us here to help you. And I . . . *we* are the greatest moonlight catchers in all of Warybone!"

Sorka jolted. She cracked a shadowy smile.

Trick crooked his head, his black eyes serious as they locked on Sorka. "And as her apprentice, you need to call to the magician."

THE MAGICIAN—
OH SO QUIETLY

A faraway whisper slipped through the tower room, soft as a feather at the magician's ear. Hushed as moonlight falling and silver flowers unfurling.

seleneseleneselene . . .

She turned to the mirror and the darkness beyond its gray surface. In the glass, a shadow hovered—a blur of long hair, black eye sockets set in a pale face, teeth flashing white.

The girl had come to her. Oh so quietly.

"Sorka," the magician said.

"Selene," came the girl's distant reply.

And there it was—the magician's name. She had forgotten it, but for now at least, it settled in her mind. Uncomfortably. Something that no longer fully belonged to her. It had fallen away like so many other things that had once seemed important.

"I grew weary with waiting." The magician blinked heavy eyelids. All the sleep she'd lost. All the magic she'd spent.

All of Warybone breathing and breathing and breathing so loudly.

The magician frowned. "What has kept you away?"

Sorka's eyes flitted to the side, gazing at something beyond the mirror's frame. She gathered herself, then—a rolling back of her shoulders, a sharp set to her shadowed jaw. "It is not the same." She turned back to the magician. "Being here"—she spread her hand to take in the whole of the darkness—"and being there."

Warybone.

"Doubtful," the magician said, for she'd magicked the darkness in its likeness.

"Truthful," Sorka said. "The darkness is being most disagreeable."

Sorka reached out one hand as if she might slip it through the mirror, but it was only a looking glass and allowed no passage to Warybone.

The magician shook her head. "My devil, my dear, tell me. Are you tending the darkness?"

She leaned her face so close to the glass that fog bloomed where her lips nearly touched the mirror's surface. And she could see very well that the girl had not taken care. The edges of the darkness curled closer, like a knot tightening.

Sorka retreated, a small step back. Her form grew less distinct. A vague outline of a shadowed girl. "Come," she beckoned. "Come and tend it."

The magician felt one slow beat of her absent heart.

30

AT TORCHSET

Sorka stumbled away from the gilded-framed mirror, joining Rooney and the others among the trees. Her eyes had gone glassy. Her lips twitched into a smile.

"Will she come?" Rooney asked, clutching her lunar mirror protectively.

"Oh, she'll brave it! I know she will." Sorka circled around Trick. She pranced by Devin. She wiggled her long nose at Bridget.

"Then I might return home by suppertime." Devin looked up, but there was no telling if daylight or nightfall claimed the world above. "Or maybe breakfast?"

"How can you be sure she'll come?" Trick held his lunar mirror too, as if he were ready to point it at the sky right then, should the magician make a sudden descent.

"Because." And that was all Sorka would say.

It was not helpful in the least, and Rooney suspected

Sorka still had a secret tucked away behind those pale lips, not yet ready to tell them all her truths.

"*When* will she come?" Bridget asked, tracking Sorka's romping with her sharp green eyes.

"When everyone else sleeps. When she can stand being away from . . . the darkness . . . no more."

Rooney's skin prickled with anticipation. She was about to accomplish all she'd set out to do. And she would not have to do it alone. She *could not* do it alone. "Remember, we need a mirror for Devin too."

"Oh?" Distracted and humming, Sorka flitted between the trees.

"I want to help," Devin said. "I need to—for my parents to be proud that I found my way home. So they will realize I can choose my own path. One that is right for me."

Sorka stilled at Devin's heartfelt words, as though she understood them completely. Without reply, she walked purposely over to a narrow tree, and with her arm swinging low, she slipped her hand into a shadowed hollow all but hidden behind a pile of odds and ends near its base. She scooped something from the depths. When she straightened, she tossed the object to Devin, who gasped as she caught it.

Devin looked at the mirror in delight, the very thing she'd dreamed of, gifted to her when she needed it most. She glanced shyly at Rooney and Trick. "Will you show me how to use it?"

"I said I would, didn't I? Might as well learn from the best."

Trick grinned, and Devin squealed. (A high-pitched sound that resembled the shrieking of her bow against the strings of her violin.)

Rooney had never seen Devin so happy, so she ignored Trick's teasing boast. But with the magician's return approaching, they had no time to spare, not even for a moment as special as this one. "But first, we have to ready the children."

With Sorka in the lead, they marched through the woods toward the clearing. She sang (of course she sang) a little tune not quite as creepy as the other. It stirred something in Rooney—in all of them, by the looks of the soft smiles curving their lips.

A shared glimmer of hope.

The second time Sorka started the song, Rooney and the others joined in—even Bridget, whose low voice hushed through the woods. They stumbled over the words, which made the singing all the more fun.

Come out, my devils
Come out, my dears
Hear what whispers
From the gilded mirror

The magician is coming
She'll fall from the sky
And we must be quiet
So quiet, and so very sly

Let's all play a game
Of hide-and-sneakiness
And on pale moonbeams flee
The plentiful darkness

The children came running, questions tumbling from their mouths, and Sorka spoke over them, sharing what Rooney had planned for them to do. "At torchset, when you should be shut-eyed and sleeping, we'll sneak to the woods. Every last one of us."

They listened, as if to a story, one they did not trust as true but enjoyed all the same. Rooney thought they would play along, as they always did. They would follow their (un) sullen queen, not because they feared her or were magicked to do so, but because they loved her.

Rooney looked at all their gray-splotched faces, which would soon have moonlight dancing upon them.

She could not let them down.

∾

And so, at torchset, the children gathered in the blackened woods with another stern warning that they must remain absolutely quiet and so very still. And they were, lips clamped tight and their feet silent, as always, on the silken ground. They pressed against the trees like another layer of bark, making a wide circle around the space where Sorka had last met the magician.

Sorka stood there again. Alone and waiting, the ribbons loose in her hair, the locket dangling from her hand.

The only lights shone so very dim, a sliver of moonglow from the nearly empty lunar mirrors. Clutching them tight, Rooney, Devin, Trick, and Bridget huddled together, skin dappled in shades of blue and gray.

"Hold your arm steady and true," Rooney instructed Devin before they all separated, one last piece of advice in case Trick had not said so. "Moonlight falls from so far away and takes a long while to reach us."

"I will do my best," Devin said, voice shaking with excitement or nerves. Maybe both.

"That is all any of us can do." Rooney knew Devin might not catch even a smidgen of moonlight. It seemed a simple thing, but it was no easy task capturing those wispy blue beams.

Devin slipped away, swift through the trees, and Bridget sneaked off in the opposite direction, a curt nod given in parting.

Rooney hesitated, lingering there beside Trick, the Monty at her heels. She didn't know what would happen when they returned to Warybone. If they might go their separate ways again, or if she might truly be welcomed by the roughhouse boys. Either way, she thought she ought to say something more to Trick here and now.

He took one step away from her, and she caught hold of his sleeve. He cast dark eyes over his shoulder.

Rooney's heart thumped and thumped. She didn't know if she was more nervous to face the magician or to speak these next words to Trick. "I'm sorry too," she whispered.

"I know," Trick said, though she hadn't revealed what she was apologizing for.

She wondered if she ought to explain more, but he smiled crookedly through the gloom. Maybe that's all there was to say. Maybe he'd already forgiven her.

Rooney found herself smiling back. They stood there a moment, those silly expressions on their faces, until her heart settled. And perhaps Trick's had too.

It was nice. *He* was nice.

"To Warybone," she said at last.

"To Warybone," he repeated, and they ducked into the trees, waiting for the darkness to splinter.

31

AN INKLING

The darkness pulsed by the slightest degree, a weak heartbeat. Shadows shifted. The air heavied in Rooney's lungs.

She braced herself against a tree and craned her neck, staring up, up, up at the crackling sky. It split open, a faint glow of light. The moon and pinprick stars spotted the field of pitch. Somewhere nearby, a child gasped and just as quickly smothered it.

Rooney stared and stared at this tiny pocket of the world above—and the shadowy figure stealing into the darkness on a beam of moonlight.

The magician!

She descended like a spider on a thread of silk. *And why wouldn't she?* Rooney thought. For the magician had spun this quiet place into being, trapping all the children in her web.

Cold pressed in. Rooney shivered against the tree trunk,

worried her plan might not work—worried the magician would peer down and see her if she made even the smallest movement.

But Rooney couldn't stand there doing nothing.

The Monty tugged at her bootlaces, a reminder to hurry. She opened the silver case and lifted her arm, angling her mirror just so. And she knew Trick and Bridget and Devin were hidden elsewhere in the woods, set on gathering the moonlight.

Ghostly light spiraled down. The magician dropped lower from the sky, until finally, she set her boots on the ground. Wrapped three times around her wrist, the moonbeam glowed—her magical connection to Warybone.

"You came," Sorka said, and even at a distance, Rooney could hear the note of gladness in the words. Perhaps Sorka had feared she might let everyone down too, only it seemed something more than that. Sorka leaned toward the magician; she looked up at her the way Devin had gazed lovingly at the mirror.

An uneasy knot bunched up in Rooney's belly.

"Yes, I came. I cannot fix what's broken by way of the gray-glass mirrors," the magician said, looming over Sorka and reaching out one bony hand to catch the falling ice-flowers. Her voice slipped like skates across ice. "Winter is not where I left it."

"Some things can't be fixed." Sorka clutched her crackled-glass locket. "No matter how strong the magic. No matter how fierce the wish."

Rooney tried not to let these words cloud her head. They were meant for the magician, not for her. Rooney *would* fix things. She tipped the lunar mirror forward more intently, anxious to collect the first drop of moonlight.

The magician lowered her arm, grazing her fingertips against one of the unruly ribbons in Sorka's hair. The shiny ends lifted at her touch, looping over and around each other, tying into a too-perfect bow.

Rooney faltered, nearly dropping her mirror before she steadied herself. The darkness tingled against her cheeks, little snaps of static.

Magic brewed in the air.

"This . . ." The magician threw out her arms and then drew them in, a strange embrace of the darkness. "This much, I control absolutely."

"It's all make-believe." Sorka paused, then grasped for the magician's hand. "Won't you take me home with you?"

Sorka likely hoped to draw out the conversation, to give Rooney and the others more time to gather the light, but the question hung there, strange and out of place.

An itch, an inkling, poked around in Rooney's head. How closely Sorka and the magician were acquainted. How deeply their bond might run. Master and apprentice—and perhaps something much more.

"Take you home?" The magician's face went very white, a stricken frown pulling down the corners of her mouth. "Never."

nevernevernever . . .

The pronouncement echoed through the darkness.

The magician scanned the wintry trees, her eyes sweeping right past the spot where Rooney stood. Rooney yanked back her hand, holding the mirror tight—still empty of moonlight. A panicky feeling fluttered in her chest.

She needed to find a better angle. A true line to the sky. And fast.

She peeked around the other side of the tree and raised her arm once the magician returned her attention to Sorka. The mirror pulled and pulled at the moon, its surface rippling, but not a trickle of light fell upon the glass.

Rooney hoped with all her heart that the others were having better luck. For once, she was not thinking of who might best her.

The magician murmured softly, asking winter to sleep, to stay where she'd first cast it. The darkness pulsed, like a clap of suppressed thunder. The air constricted.

For a moment, Rooney could not breathe.

She could not even hold up her arm.

At her feet, the Monty turned a dizzy circle. Its ears flattened against its skull. In the woods, the trees lurched—Trick and Devin and Bridget, the other children too, shuffling when they should have been still—all of them thinned of air.

Rooney slumped against the tree. Her hazy eyes fell on the magician.

Long strands of hair whipped wildly around the magician's shoulders. Her cloak flapped silently. She opened her mouth wide, pointed teeth flashing, and let out a long exhale.

Great coils of black fog writhed up from the magician's throat. They twisted thick and untamed, forged in the very depths of her dark heart. An outpouring of magic. It swirled through the treetops, shadowing the branches. Blowing back the sharp sprinkling of dark snow.

But the darkness itself resisted. A broken thing like everything else here.

The ground beneath Rooney quivered, and the sky above her quaked. Its edges shivered, fog coiling closer instead of expanding the darkness.

The magician swayed on her feet, clutching at the ribbon of moonlight around her wrist as though it were the only thing keeping her standing. Her mouth clattered shut. Spent of magic, of strength, the magician puffed a last curl of fog out of her nostril. Sorka reached out one helpless hand.

The darkness closed in, crouching around them.

Then its very fabric shuddered.

Rooney toppled to the ground. The pitch pressed around her, a weighted thing. Bending the long spines of the trees. Squeezing the air. Crushing the precious light.

The moonbeam recoiled, shooting up toward Warybone.

Whipping the magician away with it against her will. Her mouth formed a silent scream.

"No!" Sorka shouted. The locket dropped from her hand.

A cry tore from Rooney's throat too. She struggled to her feet. Somewhere, somewhere, Devin shrieked.

Not even the magician could tame the darkness.

Desperate, Rooney swept up her arm again, holding her mirror in just the manner she always did. *What if the moon never shows its bright face again? What if this is our only chance to gather its light?* They could not be left behind.

She strained and pleaded with the moonlight. Oh, how she tried!

But the darkness was simply too thick. The distance was simply too great. Warybone may as well have been a million miles away—out of reach.

The glow from above dimmed as the magician swept higher—as she became no more than a speck in the sky.

Something churned inside Rooney. Not the moonlit fire that sometimes filled her with hope. No, this swell of emotion fumed foul and stormy.

If she opened her mouth—if she screamed at the moonlight for abandoning her when she needed it most—she might spew out a mist as black as the magician's dark fog.

THE MAGICIAN—
A QUIET PLACE

The magician crashed onto the streets of Warybone. She gasped, limbs trembling as she stood. The moonlight no longer circled her wrist.

This much, I control absolutely.

She'd thought it the truth. She'd thought she could calm the darkness (and Sorka's tender heart). It should have been endless and beautiful, a dark mirror of the world above. A quiet place.

But she'd somehow polluted the magic—pinching tighter an already too small space.

The magician lifted her silken scarf, holding it so carefully. Despair lined her face. Her magic, her lovely magic, hadn't been strong enough.

And not for the first time.

Taking slow steps, she retreated to the Tower of Thistle. Its gold-speckled roof shone star-bright.

She could call down the moon, the stars too. The darkness should have been hers to command.

More so, to tend.

Along with all who resided within it.

32

GUTS AND GRIT

The dark fog circled, a vicious, coiling mass.

Directly beneath its swollen belly, Sorka stood frozen.

Trick broke away from the warped trees. He called Sorka's name.

With the Monty scrambling around her ankles, Rooney staggered toward them, her wary eyes on the tumultuous not-sky. Devin and Bridget too tore out from their hiding places, herding the children away through the creaking trees.

"Sorka!" Rooney shouted, for all the good it did.

Sorka watched the strange storm that had cast the magician back to Warybone, transfixed by its swirling. "Oh no." The words fell broken from her mouth. Rooney could almost *see* them, formed in the smoky fog. "She's gone."

Gathering closer, the mist scratched through Trick's hair,

a tangible thing, like creeping vines and claws. "And we better get out of here too. Come on."

He tugged Sorka's hand. On shaking legs, she stumbled forward.

Scooping the Monty into her arms, Rooney reached for the fallen locket, shoving it into her pocket before tucking in at Sorka's other side. Together, they ran through the thick, strangling air that seemed ready to swallow them.

And it would, it *would*. It ate the trees one after the other. A mouth of darkness consuming everything in its path. The trees were pulled up by their silken roots. They tipped and timbered, falling without sound before being sucked into the void.

Every branch and thread of them *gone* but for a scattering of tarnished petals.

Rooney blinked and blinked. It was impossible, and all the same, it was real.

"Faster!" she exclaimed, pumping her legs more furiously against the chill at her back. The quicksand hand of the fog. "Or it will be our end!"

"Like spring." The words gasped from Sorka's mouth. She tripped over them and her own two feet. "Gone forever."

Trick righted her before she could tumble to her knees. He held her steady as they raced on.

"You have to stop it," Rooney said, panting and frantic. She dared another look over her shoulder.

Behind them, the trees thrashed. They unraveled, limb by limb, then vanished.

"I will only make it worse!" Sorka screeched, and the roiling fog reared at the sound, drawn to her.

"Calm down," Rooney cautioned, although it seemed a silly thing to say. Her own heart beat wild and uncontrolled, just as it had when she'd first plunged into the darkness and been caught by the black vein of the river.

They neared it now, a glimmering ribbon winding through the trees. If they did not change direction, they would reach its edge and be stuck between the silken bank and the hungry fog.

Trapped.

Or maybe *saved*!

"To the river!" Rooney shouted, a half-formed idea in her head.

Trick shot her a sharp, questioning look. One she'd never seen directed at Bridget, who he trusted absolutely. Rooney glanced away only to turn back again.

"You said . . . I was one of you." She had to know if he'd really meant it. Their eyes locked as they ran. "Don't give up on me now, Trick Aidan."

Oh, it was very dark, but Rooney was looking very keenly. Trick's cheeks reddened as he said, "I'll give up on you never, Rooney de Barra."

And so they ran as they'd never run before, together.

Devin's and Bridget's swift figures, and the children's stumbling forms, shot through the trees ahead of them.

The fog cycloned at their backs, gouging the woods.

"Devin! Bridget!" One-armed, Rooney gestured frantically. The poor Monty squirmed in her other hand.

At her urging, they veered for the river of darkness. For its deep waters. Its calm.

Devin and Bridget reached it first, the children soon after. They stopped dead at its very edge.

The fog raged overhead, swirling closer and closer.

"What mad plan have you brewed up like that witch?" Beneath those stick bangs, Bridget's eyes goggled.

Rooney barreled forward. Despite the pinch of fear, she did not even slow. "Hold your breath!" she cried, and, gulping in a lungful of air, she collided with Bridget, whose flailing arms snagged on Devin.

"Ahhh!"

They tumbled backward into the water that had once almost drowned Rooney. Before her head dipped below the surface, Rooney looked up and up and up at the fog-blurred not-sky. It swarmed black as Trick and Sorka and the children leaped too.

Their bodies splashed. Their heads went under. They sank and sank in the darkness.

Everything was perfectly quiet and so very calm.

Then the river pulsed, struck from above by the magical storm.

Rooney's bones rattled. A bubble of air popped from her mouth. Waves rocked the river, tossing everyone all about, and a deep cold set in.

She held her breath as long as she could, and only when she thought she might burst did she carefully kick her way to the surface. She spun a circle. Trick popped up beside her, the Monty nosed its way from the depths, and one after the other, so did the rest of them.

A thin fog skimmed the water. It obscured much of the shore, but through it Rooney could see a looming wall of rippling darkness.

She only hoped it came no closer.

"You saved us from the void." Devin paddled to Rooney, cracking a thin lace of ice that had formed. "But how?"

"The water is magical." Rooney gathered her breath. "I just hoped it would dry up the fog the way it so quickly dries our skin and our hair."

"You didn't *know*?" Devin squealed as she swam.

"But it worked," Trick said around a splash of water. He had trusted Rooney when it mattered most.

They all had.

When they waded to shore—hair, skin, and clothes drying as their feet touched land—Rooney could more clearly see all the damage left in the wake of the magic. Frost-touched trees, a crust of silver ice-flowers, and that wall of impenetrable darkness where this sliver of the woods once reigned.

"The darkness feels *different*," one of the children said uncertainly, peering up at the crimped not-sky.

Sorka stood apart from them, so her voice came softly when she said, "Yes, little devil, that's because summer is gone forever now too."

33

ONE AND THE SAME

That night, they slept in the overlap of winter and autumn, amid the darkness that had devoured summer—and the lighthouse and sea along with it.

Or at least, Rooney *tried* to sleep, tucked tight between Trick and Devin, with the Monty behind her knees. But in the deep quiet, one of the children cried out.

Rooney slipped from her silken bedroll, for this whimper seemed worse than most. She tiptoed around those still sleeping, toward the small glow of moonlight that suddenly sputtered to life.

Sorka bent over a boy in his bed, and when Rooney knelt beside them, she realized it was none other than the little ragamuffin who'd snitched the grimace fruit from the Monty. All they had left from summer.

He lay on his back, eyes squeezed tight. A low moan rolled in his throat.

"I don't know what's wrong with him," Sorka whispered, placing one hand to his forehead.

Rooney leaned closer. His eyes flashed open, glassy and dark. Across his cheeks, crackling up and down his scrawny arms, those stains of gray-dark spread. He opened his mouth, and Rooney rocked back on her heels.

His tongue had most horribly blackened.

"I don't feel so well." He tucked onto his side while Rooney and Sorka looked at each other grimly. "Just want to sleep."

"I'll stay," Sorka told him.

Rooney nodded, knowing he'd rather have Sorka there than her. But when Rooney crawled back into her bedroll, when the moonlit candle snuffed out, darkness swarmed. It consumed the night, and she realized, next it would consume that boy. They'd thought those splotches of gray were markers of death, and this rascally boy, it seemed, would be the first to fall to them.

Rooney couldn't—she *wouldn't*—let that happen.

It wasn't a matter of when—they needed a plan for escape *now*!

Oh, her thoughts raced. They roared so loudly.

It is not the same. Being here and being there. These words of Sorka's circled in Rooney's head. A reminder.

Summer *wasn't* gone, not really. Neither were the moon and stars.

They waited in the world above.

And the world above waited for Rooney.

But how, *how* were she and her friends to reach it before it was too late?

And then a terrible, frightening, *brilliant* idea struck Rooney, like the blue beam from the lighthouse swinging round and shining upon her. Its glow chased her into dark, dark dreams.

～

Rooney, not for the first time, was the last to rise, nuzzled awake by the Monty. She bolted upright just in time to see Sorka marching away from the boy who'd fallen so ill, then stride into the woods that remained. Trick, Devin, and Bridget sat in the torch glow, watching her go.

"We're stuck," Bridget said. "That's it. That's all. We're stuck in this witch-darkened place."

"Until it smothers us," Devin whispered, her voice low so the children wouldn't hear.

"Yes." Rooney's lips twisted, more smile than frown.

Startled, three pairs of eyes swung to her.

"Why do you sound happy about being smothered?" Oh, Trick must have known something was up. His gaze bored into her.

And so Rooney told them her terrible, frightening, brilliant idea, which, in truth, sounded even worse than she imagined when spoken aloud.

"Last night, we failed to escape because the distance from

the ground to the sky was simply too great. Like the light from the lighthouse at its farthest rotation. Too distant to see. We need to bring Warybone within reach in order to grasp the moonlight." She paused before spilling the best and worst part. "We must continue to shrink the darkness."

Devin twisted her braid. "That only sounds like a way to smother us *sooner*."

Trick clenched his hands in that curious way of his, wrestling, it seemed, with the need to be bold and the need to be cautious.

But Bridget grinned, stretching the lovely little fishhooked scar on her lip. "It just might work."

Oh, Rooney had something in common with Bridget after all—the two of them were made of guts and grit. Rooney could have hugged her (but she didn't). "It *will*."

"*Might*," Bridget said again. "Moonlight is fickle and fleeting."

"But stardust isn't." Trick must have been thinking of his mother's wedding ring, created, so said his father, by the light of a star.

Devin's hands dropped to her lap. "If only its power was more than a story."

"What if it *is* more than a story?" Rooney fumbled in her pocket, withdrawing the locket, which Sorka had lost a second time.

All their eyes brightened, tracking the back-and-forth swing of the charm that Sorka claimed once held stardust.

"Then we've got to figure out how to catch it for ourselves." Bridget grinned.

Rooney inspected the locket every which way, saddened that the glass was cracked so terribly. She imagined there must have been something special about the mirror at one time, but she couldn't figure out what it might have been.

"There is only one moon, but there are so many stars in the sky," Trick said thoughtfully. "Maybe a mirror can't focus on them all at once."

"And moonlight is not the same thing as stardust, so perhaps there is another way to catch it," Devin suggested.

"Yes, yes." A burst of excitement tingled through Rooney. Trick and Devin were onto something. "Think how the stars twinkle and glow and tease—too many of them for one mirror to capture."

Just as Rooney, alone on the streets of Warybone, had felt when she encountered the roughhouse boys. Terribly outnumbered.

But she was no longer.

"Come on." Rooney climbed to her feet, then strode forward with her friends.

Scrambling along beside them, the Monty chittered, as if to encourage their feet faster. They followed the path between the trees where Sorka had gone, but not far, and soon stumbled upon the silken river.

And the rippling wall of darkness that had swallowed so much of the woods.

Sorka paced before it, eyes on the ground. She poked at the ice-flowers with a branch.

"Looking for this?" Rooney held up the locket.

"You found it!" Her smile was so wide it looked like her face might crack.

"Yes, I know how important it is to you." How important its secrets might be to all of them. "How did it ever hold starlight?"

"I don't know exactly. My mother was the one who best understood the night sky. Not me." Eyes on the locket, Sorka held out her hand.

Reluctantly, Rooney returned it. There was nothing more she could learn from it anyway. The silver chain glinted as Sorka wrapped it three times around her fingers.

Rooney froze.

She thought of how the magician descended into the darkness on a moonbeam coiled thrice around her wrist. How the magician would have to know all about the stars and moon to be able to do so—just as Sorka's mother *best understood the night sky*.

Could they be one and the same?

Everything aligned in Rooney's mind at once. That inkling she'd had about a deeper connection between Sorka and the magician. The wistfulness in Sorka's voice when they spoke. How the magician breached the darkness because Sorka asked her to, and all the many toys and trinkets and games left as gifts to please her. Even the matching ribbons they wore and their long, dark hair spoke of their secret bond.

And of course, the magic flowing in their veins.

Take me home *with you*, Sorka had said.

"I can't believe you didn't tell us," Rooney exclaimed. "You are more than the magician's apprentice—you are the magician's daughter!"

All eyes fell on Sorka. Behind her, the ice crackled at the edges of the river. In her hair, the ends of the black ribbons waved. Perhaps Rooney should have spoken more gently, but it was too late now. The darkness churned like Sorka's temper. A deepening cold bloomed in the air.

"That's the truth of it." Sorka bit off each word, a stubborn set to her gray-splotched jaw. "Now you know why I am so very rotten."

"Selene," Rooney whispered, remembering the name Sorka had used to call the magician down from her tower—*the Tower of Thistle.* "Selene and Sorka Thistle."

Devin ignored Rooney's mumbling and spoke softly to the magician's daughter. "You aren't rotten. Don't say that."

"Maybe she is." Bridget crossed her arms against the chill. "She lied to us. And anyway, she couldn't have been up to much good if she was tossed here by her own mother." She narrowed her eyes, which gleamed with curiosity. "What *were* you up to?"

Sorka scratched at the gray spread across her collarbone. "Getting into loads of trouble."

"That makes you no different from us," Trick said, as if he could see the inner workings of someone's heart, all the shiny bits and the scuffed-up pieces—a patchwork of goodness and mischief.

But Rooney knew Trick's words didn't quite tell the whole of it. Sorka *was* different—in the very best way.

Sorka had magic.

"The magician is powerful, but so are you." Rooney looked intently at Sorka. "You can bring down the sky—and the magician with it."

Sorka trembled. The darkness pinched, and the spindly tips of the treetops bowed.

"How?" Sorka asked, and Rooney told her the terrible, frightening, brilliant plan.

31

AN UN-TENDING

They schemed for hours, imagining the ways they might bring down the darkness and split open the seam. And the ways it might squish, squeeze, and smother them.

But for all their plotting and preparing (for all Bridget's pointed questions and Devin's kindly pleas), Sorka refused to explain why the magician had gifted her own *daughter* (and the rest of them) to the darkness.

"I won't say, so stop asking," Sorka said with finality.

Rooney frowned at Trick, suspicions swirling, but he was too busy plotting the best formation for gathering starlight (the cluster of them standing together with their mirrors, he thought).

For the next few nights, Sorka called to her magic—in front of them for the first time, not hidden in the woods.

Just a bit. Just to practice. They did not want her to bring the darkness down all at once and smoosh them. She needed to control it, as best she could, at least.

So in the clearing, she tugged at a corner here, a treetop there, snips and snaps of blue light rippling from the magic-infused mirror in her locket. And her emotions. She let the darkness cinch around them—an un-tending of what was supposed to be tended.

The gaps between the trees narrowed as their roots slithered over and around one another. Even the river changed course. Drawn closer, it trickled right past the throne.

The children sat quiet and obedient, eyes wary as the space around them grew smaller.

And smaller.

And smaller.

It was most unsettling, Rooney thought, to *see* the shrinking. To stand perfectly still and watch the black ribbon of the river slip inch by inch nearer to the tips of her boots. To glimpse the treetops hunching overhead, less room for their branches to stretch.

Rooney pushed her fear to the back of her mind (though it tickled there for all the days that followed), and at torchset on the seventh evening, Sorka declared, "I've made a mess of the darkness." That's just what they'd intended, but she seemed a little surprised that she'd managed it.

"A perfect mess," Devin said. "Are you ready for what comes next?"

"Are *you*?" Sorka asked.

Bridget stuck her hands on her hips. "So long as you don't witch-wallop us into the void."

"No guarantees." Sorka grinned.

They turned to the woods where that wall of darkness waited—and thrashing behind it, the black hole.

"Whatever happens, we're in this together. The best"—Trick elbowed Rooney as he finished—"and the worst of us."

"Hey!" she cried, reaching out to swat him. But he took off, Bridget and Devin on his heels.

"We'll round up the children," he called over his shoulder, laughing.

Rooney found herself laughing too, despite the fear, despite the shadows pressing in all around them. And she knew that's just what he'd wanted.

Sorka started off in the other direction, and Rooney swung back to her. "Wait, I'll come with you."

"Because you still don't trust me," Sorka said.

"Because no one should be alone." The words rang in Rooney's bones, spoken as much for herself as for Sorka. She'd been so long without her parents. She'd pretended she didn't need anyone else.

But she did.

And so they entered the woods together, their lunar mirrors—almost empty—glowing blue between them. They had to go single file where the trees pinched close, and it was there, when all Rooney could see of Sorka was the back of her head and the sway of her hair, that Sorka whispered, "Did you mean it?"

"Mean what?" Rooney asked.

Sorka slipped between the trees. She pushed low-hanging branches out of her way, and flowers drifted to the ground, leaving a silver trail of ice-petals for Rooney to follow.

"That no one should be alone." Sorka's words haunted the air, a cold breath left in her wake.

"Yes, I meant it." Passing through the cold, Rooney shivered. "How long were you down here by yourself?"

Sorka made no reply.

"It must have been lonesome." Rooney remembered when she'd first fallen into the darkness. How terrible it would have been to wander and wander and find not a soul.

Sorka walked faster through the trees, away from Rooney's words. Rooney raised her arm, holding back a swinging branch that would have otherwise smacked her in the face. And that's when it hit her (an idea, not a branch).

"That's why we're here, isn't it?" Rooney hurried along, catching up to Sorka and gently clasping hold of her arm. "So you wouldn't be alone."

Sorka blinked and blinked her widened gray eyes. A storm of emotions tossed within them.

It *was* true. The magician had plunged Rooney and the others into the darkness not simply to quiet them, but to keep Sorka company!

As if they each were another toy or trinket. A set of real live dolls for Sorka to play with.

Sorka leaned forward so they stood almost nose to nose. She did not say yes or no or maybe. She only said, "It's all my fault." Her chest rose and fell with the release of her burden. "Please don't tell the others."

Sorka spun away, but not before Rooney saw her face awash with guilt. Rooney wanted to tell her she shouldn't have held this secret so close. Sorka wasn't to blame for being lonesome. The magician's dark magic, her dark *heart*, was to blame.

But Rooney had no chance to tell her. The eerie void that seemed both real and dreamlike rose before them, masking the black hole beyond.

They stared at the roiling darkness, its ripples like waves ready to sweep them under. Rooney took one step back, and Sorka took one step forward.

"Careful," Rooney warned.

Ignoring her, Sorka snatched up a fallen branch and stabbed the pitch. It slid deeper and deeper into the darkness, and when she pulled back, nothing of the stick remained.

A trickle of fog leaked forth. It grazed Sorka's skin.

And her fingers, oh her fingers—the very tips of them blackened.

"Sorka!" Rooney yanked her friend back. "You're as ill as that boy!"

"I'm all right." Sorka curled her hand. "And so is he. He ate a summer-grown grimace fruit that didn't agree with him."

Had his tongue not been black, but the deepest purple?

"But the darkness isn't all right, and I'm about to hurt it much worse."

Rooney wondered if that was true. If, when they struck at the darkness, it lashed out, not to harm them but to close the holes they'd meant to gouge. To patch itself up. Rooney touched the gray on her cheek. And maybe sometimes, it happened to leave patches on them too.

Not a marker of death.

In its attempts to heal itself, the darkness, the magic, flowed wildly, latching onto whatever—whoever—was nearby.

And now Sorka was going to scratch at all the scars. She lifted her arms, cradling her locket in her cupped palms. "I wouldn't stand so close, if I were you."

Rooney retreated another few steps. "I won't be far."

Sorka tipped back her head, and when she sent her first spike of blue light skyward, it looked beautiful, guided not in anger or sorrow this time but with the skill of an apprentice magician. The magic zagged through the air, splashing light on the trees—and on Trick, Devin, Bridget, and the Monty as they approached.

Behind them, the children held tight to one another's hands, and at a distance, they stopped, eyes following the fractures of light snapping at the darkness.

And shrinking it further still.

A chill shook down Rooney's spine, equal parts excitement and fear. For as the light trickled in when Sorka pierced it, the darkness churned.

Her hair swept around her, a mirror image of her mother. And though the magician had said Sorka had learned nothing of the darkness, Rooney knew that wasn't true. Sorka understood it as no one else did.

The ground trembled. The seam split another fraction.

And a sliver of Warybone's sky glimmered above.

"Gather the stars," Rooney whispered, and she and Trick, Devin and Bridget reached their hands into their pockets and then thrust their arms skyward.

They tilted their mirrors in exactly the manner they'd practiced—aligned like a four-pointed star. Rooney did not mind the closeness right then. The bump of Trick's shoulder. The swish and tickle of Devin's braid. The knock of Bridget's elbow as she scooted the smallest bit away from the Monty. It felt just as it should, all of them bunched together.

Frail light floated down, but as it did so, the air shuddered; it squeezed.

Like a fist tightening around a beating heart, the darkness spasmed.

THE MAGICIAN—
THE QUIET
OF NIGHT

Crumpled at her desk, the magician startled awake, her absent heart racing. Magic twitched through her. The darkness called.

Her eyes flashed to her lovely black scarf, fallen to the floor beside the window. It looked more smoke than silk.

"Oh no, oh no." She lifted the scarf. She flew toward the door.

Fog trailed through her fingers as she spiraled down the tower's staircase and burst into the quiet of night.

35

A STELLAR MIRROR

The darkness thrashed; it constricted. Rooney fell against Trick. They held each other up, still reaching for the light, as did Bridget and Devin.

Rooney's arm shook. At her feet, the Monty squealed. Roots snaked underground as the earth rumbled, breaking apart the group's little formation.

But it didn't matter. Just as before, neither moonlight nor starlight had found them.

"It's not working!" Bridget cried. Rooney never thought she'd see it—Bridget's arm trembled too.

"But it has to work," Devin whimpered.

Rooney clenched the lovely lunar mirror in her hand. Empty. Useless.

The sky was somehow still too far out of reach, and the darkness around them reeled . . .

. . . as the magician crashed into it.

She descended on a twisted moonbeam. Down, down, down she came. The silken black swirled all around her. Her cloak flapped like wings. The air hissed as her body sliced through it.

"Sorka, my devil," called the magician. "Sorka, my dear."

Rooney wondered how she had not heard it before, such longing in the magician's voice for her imprisoned daughter. But why long for Sorka when she could simply release her from this quiet cage?

The moonbeam stretched and stretched, until Selene reached the unsteady ground. Without seeming to notice Rooney and the others, the magician cast her eyes around the undulating darkness, taking in its strange shape, all folded-in corners and too-near trees. "What have you done?"

Sorka clutched her locket behind her back, then sneaked it into her pocket. "I'm finding my way home."

Such a stricken look crossed the magician's face. "You'll only find your way to your grave!"

A plume of fog escaped from between her lips. It spread around her, stretching the darkness, even as Sorka tried to interfere, grasping for her mother's hands. Begging her to stop.

"Look," Trick said, his words sounding very far away, though he stood just beside Rooney. "Our plan *is* working!"

She glanced up. Somewhere inside her a dash of hope still

lingered. It reflected in Trick's dark eyes, a spark shining in their very centers.

A thin thread of light wafted down toward Trick's mirror—and no one else's.

If only the beam had not been so very weak—such a pale, wispy gold. As lovely as it was, it looked strange too.

Moonlight would have been blue, not gold.

Gold!

Rooney's arm dropped to her side. Everything within her tingled.

"Stardust," she breathed.

Devin, Trick, and Bridget stared at the light falling through the magician's encroaching fog. Maybe their speculations had been more than just fancy. One mirror alone could catch the light of the moon, and perhaps their grouping of mirrors had teased out the distant light of a star field, enough for Trick to pull down the smallest glimmer.

Yet it wasn't enough.

With only five mirrors, one of them near-shattered and snug in Sorka's pocket, they'd never gather as much as they needed.

Unless...

Rooney's heart thumped as her gaze locked on the crack in Trick's mirror.

Unless she'd been wrong.

She'd assumed the cracks in Sorka's locket meant it was

broken like all the other things Sorka had discarded. But what if the cracks in the glass were not a flaw but a function? Many facets to catch the many stars. Rooney's heart raced faster.

Trick had always seemed to gather the most moonlight, but maybe all that time—maybe *tonight*—he was catching a smidgen of starlight as well.

Rooney sucked in a breath. She had an idea, but oh, it was another terrible, frightening, brilliant one. Just thinking of it made her head feel woozy and light.

Or maybe that was the fog.

It drifted around their ankles. The poor Monty lay on its side, eyes closed. Its skinny ribs pushed in and out, but slowly. She had to hurry, before they all lost their breaths—smothered at last.

Rooney cringed but didn't hesitate. She dropped her precious mirror on the ground despite Devin's and Bridget's waving arms and silent protests—and she stomped on it with her foot.

Glass broke.

The magician's head whipped to the side, as if she'd heard even this small sound. Fog streamed from her mouth. It coiled toward Rooney, seeking her out in the darkness. A cold, cold tendril that might snake down her throat and choke all the air from her lungs.

Over the distance, Rooney met the magician's eyes. They looked impossibly dark. Entirely unreadable.

"You don't know what you're doing." In a whirl of movement, Selene Thistle swept into the sky, letting the moonbeam pull her up and away.

"Mother!" Sorka shouted, her voice shredded raw.

Rooney knew the magician would cut off their only chance to escape in a matter of moments.

Quick as could be, Rooney lifted the mirror from the ground at the same time she grabbed the sleepy rat. She laid the Monty gently in her pocket.

"Oh, Rooney, what have you done?" Devin whispered, eyes locked on the mirror.

Rooney was afraid to look.

Trick reached forward. He pried back her fingers when she could not bring herself to do it. "She's making a stellar mirror." A grin split his face. He must have suspected how special his cracked mirror was too.

Bridget wedged in closer, and the four of them glanced down. Lines and crackles like lightning ribboned the glass, but it remained securely in the silver case. With a shaky arm, Rooney thrust the mirror above her head and tipped it toward the sky.

Once, she might have wished upon the stars, but tonight she placed her faith in herself and in her friends. It lit not a moonlit fire, but a *star*lit fire inside her.

Devin gasped. Bridget and Trick staggered backward.

And Rooney beamed as bright as the gold-touched sky.

Unlike moonlight, the starlight refracted into a thousand

fragments when it kissed the glass. The very air sparkled, as if the sky had dropped to its knees. Rooney dashed forward, out of the trees and toward Sorka.

"Break the glass!" she cried over her shoulder.

One, two, three thumps of boots against metal, and the sharp crack of glass filled the night. Trick, Devin, and Bridget joined Rooney and Sorka.

Together (not at all *untogether*), they raised their arms. Sorka too with her little locket mirror. They gathered stardust! It was a sturdier substance, bright and beautiful as it streamed down.

Its sparkling reminded Rooney so much of those long-gone days when she'd gazed through her telescope, her parents beside her pointing out all the constellations. Now, as then, she felt she existed *among* the stars, not simply beneath them.

We gathered the stars for you, Rooney.

And now, catching starlight felt like her last gift to them.

"Come out, my friends!" Sorka called to the children, and they tumbled away from the trees and their long shadows.

The magician hovered above them, a smear against the starlight. She'd stopped her advance, whispering and murmuring spells that seemed unable to do what she hoped— for the darkness only sneaked closer.

The children stumbled, legs buckling as the ground shuddered and shifted beneath them. Rooney and Devin fell just after. Smooshed once again, the rat awakened and scurried from Rooney's pocket.

Around them, the darkness was reconfiguring, the rippling walls pressing in.

There was no time to spare. The whole realm might collapse around them. Rooney lifted her mirror, rejoining Trick and Bridget, who had recovered from their falls more quickly and stood with their feet firmly planted, commanding the starlight. Devin completed their small circle as Sorka faced off with the magician.

"First things first," Rooney said, looking in turn at each of her friends' fierce faces. "We must protect the children."

She reached toward the starlight. It glinted at her touch, a solid thing unlike anything she'd known before. It tickled, warm and sparkling against her skin.

Rooney grasped the golden beam. Trusting in its magic, she wrapped it three times around the closest child's wrist, and like snapping a fishing line, she sent the child reeling through the darkness, straight past the magician and into the world above. A scream of fright and delight echoed around them.

"Not Sorka, not Sorka!" The magician commanded the silken trees, the branches of which reached out like long, spiky claws. They grabbed at the children, grasping for their ankles and wrists. Some children were yanked up into the air, screaming as they dangled upside down. Others fled toward Rooney's group, where, one by one, Bridget (quickly) and

Devin (carefully) twined starlight three times around their wrists and sent them soaring skyward.

Rooney and Trick stood side by side, pulling the starlight toward their mirrors, brightening the whole of the darkness.

"Monty!" Rooney cried. "We need you!"

The smudgy rat poked its nose from between the crook of two branches. With her free hand, Rooney pointed to the children swaying from the treetops, caught there by the magician. The Monty dashed toward them, its sharp teeth flashing. Bridget and Devin ran after, climbing into the trees and reaching for ribbons of starlight.

"I can't let you devils undo the darkness." The magician exhaled another thick cloud of black fog that Sorka was unable to keep back no matter how she bent the darkness to her will.

"I can barely see," Rooney said, swiping her hand over her mirror in an attempt to chase away the fog. She looked up at Bridget and Devin, who'd secured more of the children with threads of starlight, but they hesitated, unable to determine the way out amid the fog.

Those sparks gleamed in Trick's blackberry eyes. "Can you manage the starlight alone?"

Rooney held her arm steady and strong. "Yes, yes," she said.

And with that, Trick swung himself into the nearest tree. He rose all the way up to the tip-top branches and leaped for another one angled almost horizontally above him. Higher and higher he went, past Devin and Bridget, until the darkness swallowed him.

All the while, the magician cast spells, and the fog swirled. Sorka dropped to her knees, no match for her mother's magic.

From the darkness came a soft tinkling, like rain—no—like *music*. Somewhere in the gloom, Trick must have reached the starlight above the fog, and now he strummed the cords like a harp. With each cascading note, the starlight brightened, showing them all the way out.

Bridget aimed. She sent the rest of the children soaring on beams of starlight, heading that-a-way toward Warybone. The magician swept closer, angling right for Bridget. Devin snatched her mirror from her pocket and aimed it just so, catching the scattered golden light and shining it into the magician's eyes. The magician swerved away.

"Go!" Rooney shouted, urging her friends on.

Devin found her own strand of starlight and let it carry her toward Trick's delicate notes, and Bridget seemed ready to follow her when she halted quite suddenly. The rat circled her ankles.

For a moment, Rooney worried Bridget would kick the Monty from its perch. But with a grimace and a shriek, Bridget snatched the rat up by its tail and brought it with her through the sky.

Still holding the mirror aloft, Rooney raced toward Sorka. The magician began to descend at the same time, slowly, wearily.

"Sorka," the magician wept.

Sorka looked up at her mother, then turned at Rooney's voice. "We have to hurry!"

Rooney reached out for a starbeam. It tingled as she wrapped it thrice around her wrist.

"I'm scared," Sorka whispered, a wistful expression on her gray-splotched face.

Rooney clasped Sorka's hand, which was so very cold and light. "We will go *together*," she promised.

They snapped the beam of light, and it drew them through the sky. They rose more slowly than the other children, the darkness unwilling to let Sorka go. The higher they climbed, the brighter Sorka's eyes sparkled, the lighter the touch of her hand.

Rooney felt as if she were flying. They were so close to the seam.

But closer still loomed the magician.

THE MAGICIAN—
EVER SO QUIET

The magician looked down at the dark-haired girl with the holey tights—and at Sorka.

Sorka, her devil.

Sorka, her dear, dear, dear.

The magician spread her arms wide, starting her cloak flapping, sending the fog whirling. She blocked the path. She refused to let them by.

All the others who'd gone, she'd meant them to escape, had asked the trees to release them—though the darkness had intervened. Now, the magician only cared what became of Sorka—who belonged to, who could not leave, who *had to*, *had to*, *had to* remain in the darkness, no matter how small and tangled it had become.

"I won't let you go," the magician whispered, her voice ever so quiet. Holding tight to her moonbeam, she swept lower in the sky.

The dark-haired girl shook her starbeam, as if to make it carry them faster, all the while clinging to Sorka. "You can't keep us here. Out of our way!"

Sorka said nothing. She only spun at the end of the girl's hand, feet dangling in the darkness, hair gusting away from her face. And those black ribbons, the very ones the magician had once tied prettily in her daughter's hair, streamed wild from wind-blown braids.

The magician cut through the fog and the stardust, a scattering of dark and light playing across her raw-boned face. The girl never flinched. She never slowed their ascent or let her grip on Sorka falter, not even when the magician drew close enough that the girl shivered with cold.

In the middle of the sky, they collided. Stardust tangled with moonlight. The black trees stretched for them. And peering down from above, a sour-eyed boy, a girl with a heart-shaped face, and a scar-lipped child reached through the darkness, never mind they were too far away to do anything at all.

The starbeam around the dark-haired girl's wrist unraveled by one turn, and she shrieked. A horrible sound.

The magician recoiled, only to redouble her efforts a breath later, straining to tug Sorka away. The girl kicked out her boot, sending the magician spinning. Sorka lifted out of reach. She neared the seam.

"Wait!" The magician raised her voice for the very first time. It cracked with disuse. "Please wait. Please don't go."

They didn't slow, not right away, but then, soft as silk, Sorka said, "Wait, Rooney."

The magician wasted not a moment. She commanded the moonbeam to lift her fast, fast, fast to Sorka's side.

"Please stay," she said, reckless now with her words. "Please stay. Where it is quiet. Where it is safe. In this protected place I've made for you. Oh, Sorka. I cannot bear to think of a world without you in it."

"But I'm not part of your world anymore!" The words tore out of Sorka's throat.

Tears sprang from the magician's eyes. They ran down the river of scars all her previous weeping had tracked into her cheeks. "I should have been there only for you. I should never have left your side when you grew so sick. I'm sorry. So sorry." Her voice came raspy. "The townsfolk needed me too, but you needed me most." She drew a breath. "Please forgive me."

Sorka shook her head. Her lip trembled. "Mother," she whimpered.

"I love you." The magician's absent heart swelled being so near to Sorka. It filled her chest. It ached. Oh, it ached. She'd held back these words for too long. "Do you know how much I love you?"

"I know," Sorka said. "For I love you just the same."

36

TO WARYBONE

Rooney clutched the starlight, fearful it would unwind from her wrist another turn, and then one more, spilling her and Sorka to the tree-spiked ground far below. But Rooney could not help but wonder if she would be the only one hurt in the fall.

The magician's words to Sorka fluttered in her head. *I cannot bear to think of a world without you in it.* Rooney tried to pretend that she didn't understand. That it couldn't possibly mean what it seemed.

She tugged on the starbeam, urging it to carry her higher, away from the magician, away from those words. Above, three pairs of arms stretched down. They looked overlong and distorted, breaking through the seam and straddling two worlds. Trick's hands found Rooney first, and his fingers closed around her wrist.

She clung to Sorka, but Sorka loosened her grip.

"You're slipping!" Rooney shouted.

With her other hand, Sorka reached toward the magician. Or rather, Sorka reached for her *mother*.

"Cross with me," Sorka said to Selene.

"No, no," wept the magician.

All the same, daughter and mother clasped hands. Sorka's fingers sneaked away from Rooney's tenuous hold.

"Sorka!" she cried.

Trick's voice echoed down, as if coming from the other end of a very long tunnel. "I've got you, Rooney."

Unware that she came alone, he pulled her up and away from Sorka. There was so much light as Rooney passed through the seam, and the starbeam scattered apart. It sparkled everywhere, pushing back the plentiful darkness as she spilled into the world above.

She hit the ground hard, landing face-first on the cold cobblestones. Trick was sprawled beside her, their hands still linked. He squeezed her fingers, once, so quickly, then released her.

Rooney lay there a moment, catching her breath and blinking at the boots of all the children they'd flung from the darkness. All the children they'd protected.

When Rooney rolled over, Devin and Bridget were staring down at her.

"Where's Sorka?" Devin asked, worry lining her brow.

Rooney and Trick climbed to their feet in the shadow of the Tower of Thistle. On the ground spread a splotch of the deepest darkness, speared by a single moonbeam.

Rooney didn't know what to say. She didn't know what to think. "Sorka let go of me."

"She's not coming?" Devin tipped her face over the void and wrung her hands. "But she has to."

Bridget cupped her palms around her mouth and shouted down into the pitch, "Come out, my friend! Come out, my foe!"

All the lines of that creepy song ran through Rooney's head again, and one in particular rang loudest. "It's death you've found," she whispered.

The darkness rippled. It parted. Selene and Sorka Thistle emerged from its depths, crossing together from the plentiful darkness into the starlit night.

Rooney gasped. Trick, Devin, and Bridget went rigid, perhaps struck with the very same thought as Rooney. That they'd found the truth of Sorka's secret.

Death had come to Warybone last year. The feather flu had stolen so many away. *The townsfolk needed me too, but you needed me most.* The magician had spoken so sorrowfully. Rooney's heart clenched, wondering if it was really possible that the feather flu had snatched Sorka from the magician too.

If Sorka, standing so ghostly gray before her, was dead.

THE MAGICIAN—
THE UNQUIET

The magician clutched Sorka's hand. It was cold, insubstantial, her skin as pale as moonlight.

"Is this truly what you want?" the magician asked, disbelieving.

"Most of all," Sorka replied. "And for you to keep your heart."

"I will keep you in it," Selene said, for Sorka *was* her heart.

"You have room in there for more than me. Let them in." A breeze blew past; it blew *through* Sorka. "That tickled," she whispered in awe.

Someone inhaled sharply, and Selene drew her eyes from Sorka. A grouping of children stood before them on the cobblestones, the dark-haired girl Sorka had called Rooney among them. They inched closer.

"Is this goodbye?" Rooney asked, shooting a quick, wary look at the magician before returning her eyes to Sorka.

"You know?" A small frown slipped across Sorka's face.

"We know," Rooney said.

Sorka's willowy form wisped, her fingers light as air in Selene's hand. And no matter how tightly Selene held on, no matter how she magicked her cloak of quiet closer to her daughter, none of her efforts would keep Sorka here.

"Yes, then," Sorka said. "It's goodbye."

A chorus of soft farewells sounded from all the children who loved Sorka, then Rooney spoke again. "I think that when I say your name, you will hear it. Wherever you are."

Sorka smiled.

"Wherever you are," Selene said, and when Sorka gifted her with a smile too, the magician's heart broke and healed all at once.

A shooting star streaked through the night. Sorka tilted her head. Her eyes went wide. Upon seeing the true sky, laughter bubbled up from her throat, obnoxious and loud and *wondrous*.

It shook through Selene. She let the sound wrap around her and sink into her bones. She hadn't heard Sorka laugh in so long. And strangely, it didn't hurt to hear it. Selene never wanted the laughter to stop, but it weakened, it faded, like a thunderstorm rolling past.

All the magician had been able to capture in her magical silken world was the glimmer of her daughter's spirit. And now, that too was slipping away.

"My dear," Selene said.

Sorka sighed, her last breath kissing her mother's cheek. And then—with a soft sweep of her hair in the wind and a clever curl of her lips—she was gone.

Selene shut her eyes. She folded her empty hand.

And she listened.

Not to the quiet, but to the *unquiet*—all the sounds throughout Warybone that she'd wanted to smother for so long. The ones that had reminded her too much of Sorka. The ones that had been too happy, too playful, too loud and full of life.

She breathed in time with the people of Warybone, letting her lungs expand and contract in rhythm with their own. In and in, and out.

How dare I? she thought, horrified by all she'd done.

Her eyes flashed open, and she looked at the children she'd wronged so terribly. Selene knew she must make it right—if they would let her.

37

A BLACK HEART
LINED WITH GOLD

Goodbye, Sorka," Rooney whispered.

She might have been sad (she was), but less so than she'd expected, because Sorka had done what she wanted. And that was Sorka's own rule, after all.

"She's really gone," Devin said wistfully.

"But the magician is *not*," Bridget hissed.

Rooney glanced at Trick, who reflexively tightened his hands into fists. Of course, he wouldn't swing them, but the magician didn't know that, and he looked dark-eyed and fierce next to Rooney.

From the corner of her eye, she also saw the Monty. It poked its whiskers out from the blackberry bushes. Its sharp teeth flashed, as if it were prepared to bite the magician's ankles should she try anything.

Selene stood very still and watchful. She appeared no less forbidding in her fitted black suit and cloak, except for her gray, gray eyes, which had gentled as soft as a dove's downy feathers.

Rooney didn't know what to do—to run and run as fast and far as she could, or to face the brokenhearted magician who'd spoken so lovingly to Sorka. With her friends and the rat at her side, Rooney gulped down her fear. She found the simple words she wished someone had once offered to her.

"I'm sorry." Before Trick could nudge her elbow, she added, "We're *all* sorry about Sorka."

When the magician did not utter a threat or call to her magic, Rooney raised her chin. "My parents are gone too, and I miss them very much. I couldn't protect them either." The words came swiftly, a desire to ease the sadness around her, all that still clung to her and her friends. All that cradled the magician. "Sometimes when everything goes wrong, one thing can make it a little bit better, though."

Rooney bent down, lifting Sorka's locket from the ground. With a shaking hand, she held it out to the magician. It was open a crack, shining with stardust, and maybe it echoed with wondrous notes of laughter too.

Selene accepted the locket without word, and so Rooney stumbled on. "It's very much like the lunar mirror someone left me when I needed it most."

Rooney drew it from her pocket. Moonlight caught the etching of the delicate thorn stem.

A lovely *thistle*.

Rooney looked from the silver case to Selene Thistle,

wondering, wondering at the chance of it. But it really wasn't chance at all. Her lunar mirror, and all the rest of them, must have been designed by someone who understood the night sky and magic.

"*You* gave us the mirrors," Rooney said, catching another glimmer of this unknown side of the magician, whose black heart just might have been lined with gold.

"I crafted them before Sorka fell ill." Selene's voice broke on her daughter's name, and then she admitted, "Though I called to it, my magic could not help your parents." Her gaze fell on Rooney, Trick, Bridget, and the other children standing there in the night. "But I thought it might help you in trying times."

Rooney ran her finger over the familiar groove in her mirror's case. So much care had gone into forming it. Rooney tried to align what she knew of the magician's dark ways with this unbelievable truth—that Selene had done what she could to help the town of Warybone, only to be consumed by grief when her own daughter fell to the same misfortune.

"I've behaved terribly and unforgivably," Selene said. "And I don't know the firstly thing about setting it right."

Rooney couldn't speak for the children. She could hardly speak for herself. Tears scratched at the back of her throat— for Sorka, for them all. The magician *had* done something inexcusable . . . yet once, she had also done her best to save them. One action did not necessarily balance out the other, but Rooney's heart felt very full and generous.

"You can try," Rooney said. "To set things right, that is."

"Yes," Trick agreed, the most forgiving among them. And if he saw something good inside the magician, then it must be there. "But you'll have to earn our trust."

"You'll have to make amends too," Bridget said, a grin hitching her lip and hinting that she had a good number of ideas for how the magician might do so.

"You'll have to speak with my parents," Devin said sternly, but her eyes went to the mirror in Rooney's hand, as if she wondered what the magician could teach them of magic and moonlight.

Selene stared at them with wide, startled eyes, a telling look. She must have been certain they would turn her away. "I will do anything."

"Then it's settled." But Rooney had no idea where to start.

"Firstly . . ." Selene hesitated after only one word, perhaps as unsure as Rooney.

"*Firstly*, you can witch-magic us a midnight supper," Bridget said.

"Anything but grimace fruit," Trick added, scratching his forehead. The splotch of gray spread on his temple peeled off.

"Oh!" Rooney's hand flew to her cheek. She scrubbed her skin, and the gray came away like a spiderweb swept from a corner. It seemed a good sign—that things *could* be made right.

"Come," Selene said softly. "If you want."

"We will; we do." And Rooney took the first step forward.

All the children with parents ran off into the night, finding their ways home as if they'd only woken from a dream. Devin too, though she left with hugs and promises to see Rooney and the others soon enough, bringing her parents along with her.

And those children with nowhere to go—like Rooney and Trick and Bridget (and the smudge-nosed Monty too)—they entered the Tower of Thistle alongside the magician, all of them together, finding one another when they needed it most.

THE END

ACKNOWLEDGMENTS

Thank you, readers, for plunging into the plentiful darkness. Stay as long as you like, for when you're ready, the stars and moon will show you the way home.

As for home, this book could not have found a better one than with my editor, Brian Geffen, who finds the pulse of a story and ensures it beats fiercely. No one holds a moonlit candle to your editing magic.

Last year, I gave my agent, Suzie Townsend, the name *Suzie Starlight*, which seems especially appropriate for this book too. Thank you for always guiding my way when I'm stumbling around in the dark.

Everyone at New Leaf and Holt/Macmillan has offered such support, especially Dani Segelbaum, Christian Trimmer, Liz Dresner, Rachel Murray, Allene Cassagnol, Callum Plews, Lelia Mander, Taylor Pitts, Starr Baer, Alexei Esikoff, and Madison Furr. And I am so thankful that Kaja Kajfež (Iz Ptica) beautifully illustrated the cover for another one of my books. I have so much appreciation for you all.

So many thanks to Karen Strong for reading the synopsis and early chapters of this story and providing such encouragement. To Kara Price and Sara Casiday, my oldest and dearest friends. And to Joan He, Gita Trelease, and Gabrielle K. Byrne—as the moon brightens the night sky, you all brighten my heart.

Mom, Bill, Pop, and Gram—you gathered the stars for me, and I will forever be trying to catch them for you. Cam, I would chase you into the darkness; I would chase you anywhere. Love you.